"WE GOT VISITORS . . .

Starkey woke up fast. By the time he got his hands on his own rifle, Slocum was already back at the window. Starkey moved quickly to the other window and looked out.

The riders began to move slowly, spreading out to the sides in both directions. One struck a match, and before either of the men inside could react, he touched it to a torch that flared up instantly in the darkness. Starkey flung up the window and poked the barrel of his rifle out. Slocum did the same.

"Hold it right there," Starkey called.

"Toss it," called a voice from outside, and the man with the torch swung his arm and let the torch fly. It banged against the front door and fell to the porch. Starkey squeezed his trigger, the torch thrower clutched at his shoulder and slumped in his saddle. Slocum fired and another rider slumped.

"Scatter," called the voice from outside.

Slocum fired again and so did Starkey, but the targets were moving and disappearing in the darkness.

"Are you hit?" Starkey asked.

"No," said Slocum. "I'm all right."

It was suddenly quiet. There were no more shots, no more shouted orders from outside. The silence was eerie . . .

DON'T MISS THESE
ALL-ACTION WESTERN SERIES
FROM THE BERKLEY PUBLISHING GROUP

THE GUNSMITH by J. R. Roberts
Clint Adams was a legend among lawmen, outlaws, and ladies.
They called him . . . the Gunsmith.

LONGARM by Tabor Evans
The popular long-running series about U.S. Deputy Marshal
Long—his life, his loves, his fight for justice.

SLOCUM by Jake Logan
Today's longest-running action Western. John Slocum rides a
deadly trail of hot blood and cold steel.

JAKE LOGAN

SLOCUM AT DEAD DOG

JOVE BOOKS, NEW YORK

SLOCUM AT DEAD DOG

A Jove Book / published by arrangement with
the author

PRINTING HISTORY
Jove edition / February 1997

The Putnam Berkley World Wide Web site address is
http://www.berkley.com/berkley

ISBN: 0-515-12015-4

A JOVE BOOK®
Jove Books are published by The Berkley Publishing Group,
200 Madison Avenue, New York, New York 10016.
JOVE and the "J" design are trademarks
belonging to Jove Publications, Inc.

PRINTED IN THE UNITED STATES OF AMERICA

10 9 8 7 6 5 4 3 2 1

1

Slocum rode slowly, if not wearily, and the big Appaloosa beneath him did not object to the pace either. The road behind them had been a long one, dusty and desolate, and both horse and man were looking forward to a well-deserved rest and something more than trail food. They did not pause at the sign in the road that bore the lettering DEAD DOG. They simply continued their plodding pace, but they both knew that the sign meant a town was somewhere just ahead, and that news was very much welcome. They topped a small rise, and then the town came into view.

Slocum could tell immediately that Dead Dog was not much of a town: It had one main street with a row of businesses on either side. Scattered out from there were a few houses. As he rode into the town, he thought that he could tell why it was called Dead Dog. It was small, and it was quiet. There seemed to be almost no activity. It was evening, but it was still early evening. Perhaps things would pick up later, but then, he couldn't imagine where the people would come from.

A cowboy mounted his horse and turned to ride out of town. As he passed Slocum, he touched the brim of his hat and rode on in silence. Slocum saw a sign that read DEAD DOG SALOON, and he pulled up and dismounted in front of a hitching rail. As he slapped the reins around the rail, he noticed a hefty man lounging against the outside wall of the saloon.

"Howdy, stranger," said the man. He was picking at his teeth.

Slocum glanced up, and only then did he notice the badge pinned onto the man's vest. He nodded and touched the brim of his hat, then stepped up on the boardwalk and headed for the front door of the Dead Dog Saloon. He had several things to do, but first things first. He wanted a drink. He was just about to go inside, when the lawman spoke again.

"Anything I can help you with, stranger?" he asked.

Slocum glanced at the man, a curious look on his face. "Not unless you want to buy me a drink," he said. "That's all I'm fixing to do. Buy a drink."

"I'm Hiram Dancer," said the lawman. "I'm sheriff here. You got business in Dead Dog, or you just passing through?"

Slocum heaved a sigh. It was the same everyplace he went. The damned lawmen always thought that everybody else's business was theirs. "Well, Sheriff," he said, "I'd like to get a drink, and then I'd like to find a place to sleep. I'd also like to have my horse taken care of for the night. A few miles back I had a thought that I might look for a job, but now that I've seen this town, it don't look too promising. I'll likely be moving on in the morning. Is that all okay with you?"

"Sure," said Dancer. "You're headed the right way for a drink. They got rooms upstairs too. With or without female companionship. Livery stable's just down at the end of the street, but it's closed for the night. I reckon I could take your horse down there for you though. If you don't mind."

Slocum glanced toward the far end of the street. "I'd be obliged," he said. "But lead him. Don't try to get on him."

"Oh?" said Dancer. "He a mean one, is he?"

"Let's just say he's a one-man horse," said Slocum. He stepped back down into the street and pulled the blanket roll loose from behind the saddle. He jerked the Winchester from the boot. Then, blanket roll over his shoulder and rifle in the crook of his arm, he went back to the entry of the Dead Dog Saloon and put his hands on the batwing doors.

"Enjoy your overnight stay in our little town," Dancer said, moving toward the 'Palouse.

"Yeah," said Slocum. "Thanks. I'm sure I'll have a nice quiet night here."

He wasn't surprised to discover that there were few customers in the Dead Dog Saloon. There were half a dozen cowboys, one standing alone at the bar and five sitting together at a table, and at another table were four merchant types. A saloon girl sat on the lap of one of the merchants. A woman in a matronly dress stood at the bar talking to the bartender, a big, burly fellow who looked like he could wrestle a grizzly and stand at least a fifty-fifty chance of coming out victorious.

Slocum put his blanket roll and his Winchester down at a vacant table and walked over to the bar. The bartender moved away from the woman to stand across from Slocum. He swiped at the bar in front of Slocum with a towel. "What'll it be, stranger?" he asked.

"A bottle of good Kentucky bourbon and a glass," said Slocum, "and I'll take one of them good cigars there."

The bartender put the bottle, glass, and cigar on the bar in front of Slocum, and Slocum laid down his cash. As the bartender reached for the money, Slocum said, "Who do I see about a room for the night?" The bartender paused and glanced toward the woman a few feet to his right and across the bar.

"That'd be me," she said. Slocum turned to face the woman. She stood with her left elbow on the bar, and she was looking at Slocum with a smile on her face. "Give him the key to number four, Merle," she said, "and don't take any of his money. It's no good here."

"Yes, ma'am," said Merle with a shrug. "Whatever you say."

"Veronica," said Slocum. "I'll be damned."

"It's been a long time, Johnny," she said. "You drinking alone?"

"Not now," said Slocum.

Merle put a glass on the bar for Veronica. She took it and led the way to the table where Slocum had left his things. They sat down and she poured the drinks. Slocum took a sip and enjoyed the feeling of the whiskey burning its way down his throat. He took a tin of matches out of his shirt pocket and lit the cigar.

"What brings you to Dead Dog?" Veronica asked.

"Well, what the hell are you doing here?" said Slocum.

"I asked first," she said.

"Hell, I'm just passing through," he said. "That's all. Like I told your curious sheriff, I thought about looking for a job, till I saw just how dead this Dead Dog town really is. That's all. 'Course, I sure didn't expect to find you here. Now it's your turn."

"Oh, there ain't much to tell, Johnny. After Abilene, I just wanted to get out for a while," she said. "This place was up for sale, so I bought it. It's quiet. I won't get rich, but it's a living."

Slocum sipped his whiskey and looked at Veronica over the glass. They had each been much younger the last time he had seen her, but she was still a beautiful woman, maybe even more beautiful than before. Some women were like that. They aged real well. Even in that long dress that reached from her neck to the floor, Veronica's charms were still very apparent. Her waist was still slender and her bosom ample. Her eyes were still bright, and her skin was still smooth. Slocum wondered if she had any idea what thoughts were creeping into his mind, spurred on by wonderful memories from their past lives.

"Have you had your supper?" she asked. "I can have a steak cooked up for you."

"That would sure hit the spot," he said. "I ain't had anything fit to eat for a few days. Just my own trail cooking."

"Merle," Veronica called out.

"Yes, ma'am?"

"Rustle up a steak dinner for my old friend Slocum here, will you? I'll watch the bar for you till you get back."

"Coming right up," said Merle, and he disappeared through a door behind the bar.

Across the room the girl on the merchant's lap giggled and stood up. The merchant stood and the two of them headed together for the stairway that led up to the rooms. The remaining merchants at the table laughed and made a few off-color remarks as their companion left their table. He looked back over his shoulder at them and waved a hand.

"Ah, shut up," he said.

The lone cowboy at the bar turned and looked straight at Slocum. Slocum tensed just a bit, ready for anything. He had never seen the man before that he could recall, but that didn't mean anything. He'd had a couple of close calls at the hands of strangers before. If someone had a grudge against you, he could pay a man you never saw before to do you in. And this man had the look of a man who could handle himself. He was about Slocum's size but several years younger. Veronica noticed Slocum's reaction to the man's stare.

She had seen him like that before. She put a hand on Slocum's arm.

"It's all right, Johnny," she said. Then she looked at the cowboy and raised her voice. "Come on over, Sam," she said. The cowboy walked over to the table. "Sam Starkey," said Veronica, "this is John Slocum, an old friend of mine." Starkey touched the brim of his hat. "Sit down, Sam," said Veronica.

"No thanks," said Starkey. "I'm leaving. I didn't mean to be eavesdropping, Slocum, but did I hear you say you're looking for work?"

"I think I said that I'd thought about it until I saw this town," said Slocum.

"Well, I got a ranch outside of town," said Starkey, "and I need a good hand. You interested?"

"Just like that?" said Slocum.

"Just like that," Starkey said. "You're a friend of Veronica's. That's good enough for me."

Slocum thought about his nearly empty pockets. "When do I start?" he said.

"First thing in the morning. Just ask anyone how to get to the SS."

Before Slocum could think of anything else to say, Starkey had left the saloon. Slocum looked up at Veronica. "Guess I'll be sticking around awhile after all," he said. He took a sip of his whiskey.

"That might not be such a good idea," Veronica said, her voice low.

"Why not?" said Slocum. "It looks pretty good from here."

"Johnny," she said in a near whisper, "there's a rancher here named Ben Berry. Big rancher. He's been trying to take over the whole valley. He went easy at first. Kind of sneaked up on us. He'd notice that one of the small ranchers was in trouble, and he'd offer to buy him out. No one thought much about it at first, but then he got to making offers on anything, whether the owner was in trouble or not. If they wouldn't sell, pretty soon they'd start having trouble.''

"What kind of trouble?" Slocum asked.

"You name it," she said. "Rustling. Barn burning. Cowhands getting beat up or shot at. Well, anyhow, Berry's run everyone off except young Sam Starkey."

"My new boss?"

"That's right. He's the last holdout."

"I'll be damned," said Slocum.

"If you go to work for Sam," Veronica said, "you'll be right in the middle of it."

"Meaning that he wants a gun hand," said Slocum, "not a cowhand."

"That's the way I see it."

"What about the sheriff?" Slocum asked.

"Hiram Dancer either won't do anything or can't," said Veronica. "I just don't know which, but you can forget about getting any help from him."

Slocum took a long draw on his cigar and let the smoke out slowly.

"How many hands has Starkey got?" he asked.

"Johnny," said Veronica, "he's got one. Just one, and you're it."

Slocum sat in silence, mulling over the information he had just taken in. It seemed as if Starkey had just hired him under false pretenses. He hired him for a cowhand, but he really expected to use him in his fight against Berry. Well, Slocum wasn't looking for a fight, and after his first look at Dead Dog, he hadn't really even been looking for a job. He thought about getting a good night's sleep and, after a good breakfast in the morning, riding the hell out of this place. He didn't like the idea of accepting a man's offer of a job and then just not showing up for work, but then, the man hadn't exactly told him the whole truth of the matter.

"Just move on, Johnny," Veronica said. "It's not worth the risk."

"Well," said Slocum, "that sounds like good advice."

Merle came out of the kitchen just then with a plate of food—a good-looking steak, some fried potatoes, and a hunk of sourdough bread. He put the plate on the table in front of Slocum along with a knife and fork.

"Thanks," said Slocum.

"Thank you, Merle," said Veronica. Then to Slocum she said, "Dig in."

The four cowboys at the other table got up and left the saloon, and Slocum had a sense that they were looking sideways at him as they passed him by. Merle came out from behind the bar to clean up their table.

"Good food," said Slocum. "You're running a nice place here, Veronica."

"Be nicer if there was a little more business," she responded. "But I guess I shouldn't complain. Merle's good help, and if anyone gets too rowdy, he can handle it. I don't know what I'd do without him."

Slocum glanced up at Merle. He was not a bad-looking man, big and husky for sure, but still, not bad-looking. He wondered if there was anything besides a job between Veronica and her bartender, but then he told himself that it was really none of his business. He finished his meal, and Veronica took the dishes over to the bar. Slocum poured himself another drink. He noticed Hiram Dancer come into the saloon and walk to the bar.

"Good evening, Hiram," said Veronica. She walked back to the table to sit with Slocum.

"Whiskey," said Dancer. When Merle served him his drink, he picked it up and followed Veronica. "Mind if I sit down?" he said.

Veronica looked at Slocum, and Slocum shrugged. "Sit down," he said.

Dancer pulled out a chair and plopped into it. He took a sip of his whiskey and coughed. "Slocum," he said. "That your name?"

"That's right," said Slocum.

"Well, Slocum," said Dancer, "I just heard a rumor. I heard that you found yourself a job. You told me that you wasn't looking for a job in Dead Dog. Said you'd be moving along in the morning."

"That's what I figured when I said it," Slocum said.

"It's still a good idea," said Dancer. "You go to work for Starkey, you're just going to get yourself into trouble. You know, sometimes a man's first instinct is the best. I'd advise you to follow your first instinct and ride out of here first thing in the morning."

2

Sheriff Hiram Dancer finished his drink and left the saloon. Puffing his cigar, Slocum watched him go. Then he put the cigar in the ashtray there on the table and picked up his own drink.

"That fat son of a bitch," he said.

"Don't worry about him," said Veronica. "He just likes to hear himself talk."

Slocum turned up the glass and drained it, then picked up the cigar and stuck it in his mouth. He pushed back his chair and stood up, reaching for his Winchester and blanket roll.

"I'd better turn in," he said. "Got to get an early start in the morning."

"You don't have to get out of town that fast," said Veronica.

"I've got a job," said Slocum. "I don't want to be late the first day."

"Johnny, I thought we talked all that out," said Veronica. "You'll wind up in the middle of a fight. And then Dancer—"

"It was that fat slob who made up my mind for me," said Slocum. "I was going to leave in the morning until that bastard practically told me I had to. I ain't letting him or anyone else tell me what to do. I never have, and I ain't starting now."

"Oh, Johnny," said Veronica with a heavy sigh. "You haven't changed a bit, have you? Age sure hasn't mellowed you any."

"Good night," said Slocum. "It's been real good seeing you again."

The room was satisfactory. It was nothing fancy, but it had everything he needed, and it was clean and neat. It was just what he would have expected from Veronica. He undressed and washed the trail dust off himself, using the pitcher of water and the bowl that was provided on a small table. Then he dried with a fresh clean towel and put himself to bed.

It was a softness he wasn't used to, but he enjoyed it. He was about to drift off to sleep, when he heard the sound of a key in the door lock. He sat up quickly, reaching for the Colt that was hanging on the bedpost. The door opened, and Slocum recognized the silhouette of Veronica in her matronly dress. He eased the hammer down and replaced the Colt in the holster. Veronica turned to lock the door behind her. She turned back to face Slocum, and she walked toward the bed.

"I might be dangerous," she said, "but I don't think you'll need that thing to handle me."

"No," said Slocum. "I reckon not."

"I thought you might like some company."

"Your company's always welcome," he said, and he felt a stirring in his loins beneath the sheet.

Veronica sat on the edge of the bed and took his face in both her hands. Leaning forward, she kissed him with an open mouth. He responded in kind, and her tongue darted inside his mouth and began exploring. At last she broke away from him.

"It's been a long time, Veronica," he said.

"Too long," she said. Twisting on the side of the bed, she turned her back to him. "Help me out of this dress," she said. Slocum felt for the buttons and began to unfasten the dress. He thought he'd never get to the end of the row of buttons, but at last he did. Veronica stood up and wriggled out of the dress, then the undergarments. She left them all in a pile on the floor beside the bed.

Slocum watched with fascination as more and more of her skin was bared in front of his eyes. He took in every curve and the firmness of her flesh. By God, he thought, she's an amazing woman. By rights she should have started to sag a little here and there, but he could see no such sign of age.

He was studying her rear, as round and lovely as ever, and then she turned to face him. His eyes were riveted for an instant on the soft mound of flesh underneath the dark bush tucked just between the tops of her magnificent thighs. Then he looked upward, over her still smooth, slightly rounded belly, up to the marvelous firm tits standing out like two melons, ripe to be picked.

She stepped up close to the bed. Leaning forward, she put both hands, one knee, and then the other knee on the bed. As she crawled toward him, Slocum threw back the sheet. She moved on top of his already naked body and settled down on him, allowing her full weight to press down on him, pressing as much of her naked flesh against as much of his as was possible.

He reached around her with both arms, pulled her close to him, and held her tight. She kissed his neck and his chest, and he ran his fingers through her hair. He thought that it was wonderful to hold her again, to smell her hair and her body. Then his cock jumped as if it had a mind of its own. It jumped again.

"My," said Veronica. She reached down with both her hands to find it and to hold it. It jumped again, and she squeezed it tight.

"Ah," moaned Slocum.

"Ah, yes," said Veronica.

She guided the head of his cock between the lips of her juicy sex and rubbed it back and forth, up and down. Then she moved it to just the right spot and she pressed down against him with her hips, taking in the length of his shaft.

"Oh," she said. "Oh, that's good."

She drew her knees up under her, then sat up. She smiled and looked down at Slocum. He smiled back, and she began to rock her hips, forward and back, rhythmically, slowly and gently at first, then faster and faster until she drove with a desperation.

"Ah," she cried out.

She fell forward to relax against his chest, and then she opened her lips wide and pressed them against his mouth, driving her tongue into it and probing and searching. Then she lifted her head just enough to look him in the face, and she smiled.

"God, you're as good as ever," she said.

She took hold of his shoulders and rolled, pulling him after her until she was on her back and he was on top. He put his hands on the mattress on either side of her and straightened his arms, lifting his shoulders and chest, and then he rose up until his swollen cock almost slipped out, almost but not quite. Then he shoved downward, hard and fast and deep, and he began thrusting as fast as he could.

"Oh. Oh. Oh," she said with each thrust, and her lovely melon-shaped breasts shook and jiggled tantalizingly from the pounding, right there before his hungry eyes. It was a sight to behold.

Suddenly, on the downthrust, he stopped, pressing hard, deep inside her. He waited a moment there, and then withdrew again, but slowly. He pressed downward again, still slowly, but deep. He continued this new and gentle rhythm, and he lowered his upper body to press against her breasts. He kissed her softly on her lips, still fucking gently.

Then he felt it coming, a powerful surge from deep inside him, and he knew that he could not hold it back much longer. He picked up his speed again, just a little at first, then more and more, and once again he was driving hard into her soft, wet channel, and then he felt it gush into her, again and again and again. And then, completely spent, he relaxed, pressing her down into the soft bed with the whole weight of his body.

He was lying beside her, almost asleep, feeling wonderfully relaxed. It was comfortable being with Veronica again like that. His breathing was deep and even and relaxed.

"Johnny," she said.

"Hmm?"

"I think you should ride out of here in the morning."

"You don't like having me around?"

"I love having you around," she said. "You know that. But I don't like the thought of seeing you in the middle of a fight with the odds all against you."

"I don't like that thought so much myself," he said.

"Then why don't you go?"

"You know why," he said.

"Oh, Johnny," she said. "You're so damn stubborn."

"Yes," he said. "I am."

From the directions he had been given in town, he was only a few miles from the main gate of the SS Ranch. He had gotten up early in spite of his active night, had a good breakfast, then said, "See you around" to Veronica and headed out to find his new place of employment. On his way out of town he had noticed Sheriff Dancer on the sidewalk, scowling at him.

He was reporting for work, but he was planning on giving Sam Starkey a good chewing-out for offering him a job on false pretenses. He still felt a little stupid for staying, but Veronica had pegged him right. He was stubborn, and he didn't like being run out of towns. Especially by fat-slob sheriffs. He was rehearsing in his mind what he would say to Starkey, when he heard a woman's shrill voice just up ahead.

"Stop it," she shrieked. "I mean it. Cut it out. You'll be sorry."

He kicked his 'Palouse in the sides to hurry it on around the bend in the road. There was some kind of commotion up ahead. Rounding the curve, he saw a young woman dancing around the edges of a fight. It took a moment for him to realize that it was two against one. The girl was obviously trying to get the fighters to stop. He rode closer, and then he saw that the lone fighter was his new boss.

Slocum usually let a man fight his own fights, but two against one rankled him. He rode up close, leaned over, and took hold of the nearest fighter's collar from behind. Then he backed his horse, thus dragging the man away from the melee.

"Hey," the man shouted. "What the hell? Let go of me."

Slocum kept backing away, and the man lost his footing. Slocum let go of the collar as the man fell on his back. The furious fighter scrambled to his feet and turned to face Slocum, but Slocum had slipped the Colt out of his holster and held it leveled at the man's chest. The man stopped, staring at the barrel of the Colt.

"Don't you think one-on-one is better odds?" Slocum asked.

The man continued to stare at the gun barrel.

"Yeah," he said. "I reckon it is at that."

Just then the other of the pair drove a hard right into the side of Starkey's head, knocking him off his feet.

"Oh," the woman shouted, and she turned toward Slocum. "Well, go on and stop it," she said.

Slocum shook his head.

"No, ma'am," he said. "It's a fair fight now."

Starkey got up to his hands and knees, and the other man gave him a swift kick in the ribs, knocking him over again. Slocum winced at the sight and thought that Starkey's ribs were sure enough going to be sore. One or two of them might even be broken. He was getting just a little pleasure, though, from the fight. That's what he gets, he thought, for hiring me the way he done.

When he hit the ground again from the kick to his ribs, Starkey rolled. He rolled far enough away from his attacker to scramble to his feet unmolested. He doubled his fists and raised them for another assault.

"Come on, Jo Jo," he said, "you sorry bastard. It's just you and me now."

In that pause Slocum got a good look at Starkey for the first time. His left eye was swollen almost shut, and his face was cut and bloody. Blood had run down onto his shirtfront too, and he stood a little unsteadily on his feet.

"I don't need no help to whip your ass," said Jo Jo.

"Come on, then," said Starkey, and Jo Jo rushed forward, swinging a wide right. Starkey ducked under it and drove his own right hard into Jo Jo's belly. Jo Jo doubled over, and Slocum could hear the loud whuff of the air leaving Jo Jo's lungs. Starkey stepped back and swung an overhand left down between Jo Jo's shoulder blades.

Jo Jo staggered. He was still bent over, but he did not fall. Starkey stepped in close and raised a knee fast, smashing Jo Jo hard in the face. Jo Jo straightened up from the blow, and Starkey moved forward again. This time he reached up and put his open palm over Jo Jo's face. Then he pushed, and Jo Jo fell over backward. He landed flat on his back with a loud whump, and a cloud of dust rose around him. He didn't move. Slocum thought that he wasn't out, but his lungs were likely empty.

Starkey stood uneasily over his victim. He looked toward the other man, Jo Jo's companion, still standing obediently under Slocum's Colt. Starkey gestured toward the prostrate Jo Jo.

"Take him home," he said, panting for breath.

The man looked up at Slocum.

"Well, go on," Slocum said.

As Jo Jo's partner helped him up and onto his horse's back, Starkey staggered toward Slocum. The girl rushed up to both of them.

"Why didn't you stop it?" she said, looking fiercely at Slocum.

"That's a good question," said Starkey.

"Like I said, I took the extra one out and made it

a fair fight,'' Slocum said. "I figured that was enough.''

"Hell," said Starkey, "I guess you're right."

"Well, I don't," said the girl. "I think you're a cheap—"

"Brandy," snapped Starkey. "Calm down. I won, didn't I?"

"It's hard to tell by looking at you," she said. "God, you look a mess."

"You ride on home," said Starkey. "I'm all right now."

Brandy gave Slocum a surly sideways look.

"Oh," said Starkey. "This here is John Slocum. He works for me. Slocum, this is Brandy Berry."

"Pleased to meet you, ma'am," said Slocum.

Brandy looked away from Slocum. Starkey put a hand on her shoulder and guided her toward where her horse waited.

"Go on, honey," he said. "I got to go to the house and get cleaned up. Go on now. It's all right. They won't be coming back this evening, and even if they did, I ain't alone now."

Brandy shot one last glance at Slocum. "You might as well be," she said.

3

Slocum rode with Starkey onto the ranch. The ranch house was visible from the main gate, and there was a barn and a small corral near the house. They took care of their horses, then Starkey headed for the house.

"Let me just get cleaned up a little," he said, "and then we'll talk."

Slocum watched the dirty and bloody Starkey go into the house, then he started to look over the place. It was obviously a small operation, but everything was in good shape. The house, the barn, the corral, what fences Slocum could see, all seemed to be in good repair. That spoke well for Starkey.

Slocum figured the man would never get rich, but he could make himself a decent living with a place like this, and from what he'd seen of Starkey, he would be a man who would work hard and make a go of it. Of course it would be tough trying to do that with a big man like Berry working against you, trying to run you out of business. That was a hard way to go.

Slocum pulled a cigar out of his pocket and lit it, then strolled over to the corral. Besides his own horse and the one Starkey had been riding, there were four saddle horses penned up there. Not bad-looking stock, he thought. He put a foot on the lower fence rail, leaned his arms on the top one, and puffed his smoke. He was trying to figure out just what it was about this place that didn't seem quite right. Then he heard the sound of the door slamming behind him, and he turned to see Starkey coming out of the house.

"You had your breakfast?" Starkey yelled.

"Yeah," said Slocum. "I ate."

"Good," said Starkey. "Me too."

"Pretty nice horses," said Slocum. Starkey was standing beside him at the corral fence by this time.

"Yeah," he said. "Not bad."

"Only thing is," Slocum said, "I ain't seen no cows. You got them hid somewhere?"

"No. I'm clean out just now. I bought a small herd over to Stringtown last month. They're being delivered right now. Should be here in a few days."

"Well, am I on the payroll?" Slocum asked.

"Hell, yes," said Starkey. "I told you to come to work this morning, didn't I?"

"You got no cows," said Slocum, "and your place is in fine shape. What kind of work did you hire me on for?"

"I told you them cows is coming any day now," said Starkey. "I want to be ready when they get here."

"And you're going to pay me to just sit around on my ass till they get here," said Slocum. "Is that it?"

Starkey shrugged.

"I reckon that's about it," he said. "You can ride out and look the place over. Kind of get familiar with things, you know. Hell, I didn't want to let you get away. By the time my herd shows up, there might not be anyone left around these parts who wants to work."

Slocum turned his back on Starkey and walked a few paces away. "Yeah," he said. "I reckon that makes some sense."

"Well, what's the matter with you?" Starkey asked. "You object to a few days on easy pay?"

"Naw, I wouldn't object to you keeping me here indefinitely on a goddamned allowance if that's what you had in mind," said Slocum, "but I don't believe that's your intention."

"I told you my damned intention," Starkey said. He was getting a little huffy. "I got a herd coming, and I want to be ready when it gets here."

"That little fracas I run up on this morning," said Slocum. "What was that all about?"

"Oh, that." Starkey smiled a broad smile. "Is that what's got you worried? Hell, that wasn't nothing. Old Jo Jo—that's the bastard's name—Jo Jo Darby—old Jo Jo thinks that Brandy's his girl, that's all. She don't agree, but he still thinks that if he can whip every man that comes close to her, maybe he'll be able to get her for himself. But he won't. She can't stand him. He's just a damn fool. That's what he is."

"And just what did you tell me was the name of that little girl?" Slocum asked.

"Brandy," said Starkey.

"Brandy—what was the rest of it?"

"Brandy Berry," said Starkey.

"That's what I thought you said. Seems to me like I heard that name Berry before. Seems like I heard it in town."

"Her daddy's Ben Berry," said Starkey. "He's a big rancher in the valley here."

"Yeah. That's what I heard. I also heard that he's run everyone else out of the valley. Everyone but you."

"Well," said Starkey, looking at the ground in front of him, "he's been buying up land."

"Has he made you an offer?"

"Yeah. Yeah, a couple of times. I told him I wasn't interested, and I ain't. This is my home, and I mean to stay here."

"Have you had any problems since then?"

"You own a ranch, you got problems every day, Slocum," said Starkey, raising his voice. "You ought to know that. 'Course I got problems. I've—"

"What?"

"Oh, hell. Yeah. You got it figured right. I have had trouble with Berry. I think he's run off some of my cattle in the past. I've had a few threats. I didn't tell you before, but that Jo Jo—that's his foreman. I didn't lie about Brandy. I just didn't tell you the whole truth about Jo Jo. That other cowboy with him—that was Homer Drink. He works for Berry too.''

"You know, Starkey," said Slocum, walking up close and looking his new boss in the eye, "it really pisses me off being lied to."

"I ain't told you no lies."

"Well, it pisses me off being hired under false pretenses."

"What's that mean?"

"You told me you wanted a cowhand, and you really wanted someone to help you fight Berry. That's what it means."

"All I said was I got a ranch and I need a good hand, and you agreed to it. That's all I said." Suddenly Starkey's tone changed. Again he looked at the ground, and he scuffed some dirt with the toe of his boot. He turned around and took a couple of kicking steps away from Slocum. Then he looked back over his shoulder. "You're right," he said. "You want to go ahead and ride on out, I won't blame you none."

"I ain't riding out, Starkey," Slocum said. "I just wanted you to know up front that you pissed me off the way you hired me. That's all. I'm staying because that two-bit sheriff in Dead Dog told me to get out. That's why I'm staying. But from now on, you be up front with me, or I will walk out on you. I might even kick your ass before I go."

"I got some coffee in the house," Starkey said. "You want some?"

Slocum shrugged. "You're the boss," he said. He followed Starkey into the house, where he noted that the inside was as neat as everything outside. Starkey poured them each a cup of coffee and put the cups down on the table. Both men took chairs and sat.

Slocum sipped at the hot black liquid and eyed Starkey over his cup. "You sure got a hell of a bad eye," he said.

"It would have been worse if you hadn't come along when you did," Starkey replied. "Say, how come you didn't stop the fight altogether instead of just taking Homer out of it?"

"I don't like two on one," said Slocum. "And I figure a fair fight is none of my business. So I just made it even. Besides, I was still pissed off at you, and I wanted to see you take a little more pounding."

"I guess I can't blame you for that," said Starkey.

"You sweet on that girl?"

"Brandy?"

"Yeah."

"Well, I reckon I am."

"And her daddy's the one trying to take over your ranch?"

"Well, yeah," said Starkey, "but she ain't like him."

"Maybe not," said Slocum, "but it seems to me that you sure got yourself in a ticklish situation here." Starkey only sipped his coffee. "When did you say them cows was coming in?"

"Don't know exactly," said Starkey. "Any day now. They'll send a rider ahead to let me know."

"Well, boss," Slocum said, "what do we do in the meantime?"

"I figured as soon as we finish our coffee here," said Starkey, "we'll saddle up a couple of horses and ride out over the ranch. Let you get familiar with the lay of the land, so to speak. Does that sound all right to you?"

"All right," said Slocum. He picked up his cup and drained it. "I'm ready when you are."

It was a fine-looking place all around, Slocum thought. Not big, but a little larger spread than Slocum had imagined it would be. It had good grass and good water, and if Starkey could survive the assault of Berry, he would be able to do pretty well here. A man could do a hell of a lot worse.

He thought about his own situation, drifting all those years since the end of the war. The goddamn war. Moving from one town to another, from one job to another. Hell, he guessed that he was twice as old as Sam Starkey, and what the hell did he have to show for all those years? Not a damn thing more than one good horse.

He asked himself if he could change places with Starkey, would he do it, and he couldn't answer the question. He didn't own anything, but then, he didn't have Starkey's worries either. And he wondered if young Starkey had enjoyed his life half as much as Slocum had enjoyed his, and he kind of doubted it.

Of course, it hadn't all been fun. Not by a long shot. There had been fights and scrapes with the law and lots and lots of lonely days on the trail. And the memories of the war that still haunted him after all this time. No. It hadn't all been fun.

Even so, he'd had his share of good times, good whiskey, and fine women. And he wouldn't want to give up any of it for anything. He thought about

Veronica back in town. It had sure been good seeing her again. Seeing her and— Well, it had been good.

He'd said that he was staying around because of what Dancer had said, because he wouldn't let anyone run him out of town. But he knew deep down that at least part of the reason he was hanging around was Veronica. Yes. She sure was something, that woman. He knew that he'd be pulling out again sooner or later—unless a bullet from one of Berry's men stopped him—but he wasn't in a big hurry to leave Veronica again. No. He sure wasn't. He guessed that he'd hang around for a while.

Then, too, in spite of Starkey's little ruse, Slocum was beginning to like the man, and he didn't favor the idea of leaving him to face Berry and his crowd alone. The odds were tremendous against Starkey. They weren't improved much with Slocum along for the ride, but at least the young man wouldn't be alone.

Sometimes, Slocum figured, that was all that mattered—knowing that a fella's not alone in a fight. Well, he decided that he would do his damnedest to stick this one out to the finish. He told himself that when he did decide to ride out of this valley and away from Dead Dog, he would leave young Starkey in a secure position. He sure wouldn't leave him alone, surrounded by enemies.

4

Early the next morning, at Starkey's insistence, Slocum and Starkey hitched up a wagon and saddled up Starkey's horse. Slocum drove the wagon, and they rode toward Dead Dog together. They had some supplies to pick up at the general store, and they were going to pay a visit to Sheriff Hiram Dancer. Slocum had protested that the visit to the sheriff would be a waste of time, but Starkey had said that he wanted his position to be clear and to be a matter of record with the local law.

"We're almost for sure going to have trouble with Ben Berry," Starkey had said, "and I want Hiram Dancer to know that I didn't start it."

"You're the boss," Slocum had answered with a shrug.

• • •

It was still early when the two men pulled into Dead Dog, and the town looked sleepy. There were only a couple of people on the street. There were some horses tied to hitching rails, mostly in front of a couple of eating places.

They stopped in front of the sheriff's office. While Slocum set the brake on the wagon, Starkey dismounted and slapped his horse's reins around the rail. Together the two men walked up to the door. Starkey shoved it open and stepped inside. Slocum followed.

Dancer looked up from behind his desk. His face was red and puffy, and his shirt was splotched under the arms with sweat stains. Slocum figured the man had been up most of the night with a bottle for a companion.

"Well now, just what can I do for you this morning, Mr. Starkey?" Dancer said. He gave a hard look to Slocum, nothing more.

"I just want a little talk, Sheriff," said Starkey. "I just want to let you know where I stand before there's any kind of trouble."

"What're you talking about?" Dancer said. "Just what kind of trouble might there be? You looking for trouble, Mr. Starkey? Looks to me like you've hired yourself a gunfighter."

"You know as well as I do that Ben Berry's been trying to take over the whole valley," said Starkey. "Everyone around here knows it."

"He's bought up some land," said Dancer. "There's no law against that."

"He's been able to buy the land because his crew

has driven the smaller ranchers out of business,'' Starkey said. ''When they found themselves facing total financial ruin, they gave in and sold out to him. They didn't have any other choice. Their cattle had been rustled, Charlie Storm's barn was burned, O'Connell had two cowboys beat up real bad. Hell. You know all this stuff. Berry's method is to drive a man to the edge, then make a new offer.''

''That's your story,'' the sheriff snapped. ''There's no proof of any of that, and unless you find some proof, I suggest that you keep shit like that to yourself. You go spreading stories like that around, you could find yourself in court—being sued for libel or something. And you'd lose too and have to pay through the nose.''

''I'm the lone, last holdout in this valley, Dancer,'' said Starkey. ''I do expect trouble from Berry. I've already been threatened.''

''Beat up too,'' said Slocum. ''There's the evidence on his face.''

Dancer grinned. ''I seen that,'' he said. ''I heard he got it in a fight over a gal. Folks in town have been talking about it.''

''I bet you know what gal too,'' said Slocum, ''and I bet you know who the fight was with.''

''I didn't come here to talk about the fight,'' Starkey said. ''I just came in to tell you that if there's any trouble between me and Berry, it won't be me that starts it, but I won't be run out of the valley. I mean to protect my home.''

Dancer stood up and walked around his desk to stand close to Starkey and look him hard in the face.

"Now, let me tell you something," he said, punctuating his sentences with a fat finger. "Let me tell you what it looks like to me. From where I stand, it looks to me like you're the one fixing to start up some trouble, and so you came in here to give me your sob story to throw me off guard. It looks to me like you hired yourself a goddamn gunslinger here just for the big fight you're fixing to start. Just what the hell would you need a ranch hand for anyhow? You ain't even got no cows on your place."

"I had a few," said Starkey. "Someone run them off. I reported that to you. Remember? Anyhow, I got some more coming in," said Starkey.

"Then hire some real cowhands," said the sheriff, "not a fucking gunslinging drifter. You watch your ass, Starkey. I'm telling you. I can see right through you, boy. You be real careful you don't wind up dead or in jail."

Outside, Starkey loosed his horse's reins from the hitching rail. Slocum was just about to climb back up onto the wagon seat, when Starkey spoke.

"Well," he said, "you were right about that."

"About what?" Slocum asked.

"Talking to Dancer," said Starkey. "It was a total waste of time."

"I was wrong," Slocum said.

"What?"

"You heard me, boss. I was wrong. It wasn't a waste after all."

"Why not?"

"We learned something."

"What did we learn?" Starkey asked.

"Now we know exactly where that fat son of a bitch stands on this deal," Slocum said. "I had a pretty damn good idea before, but now we know for certain. There ain't no question."

"He's backing up Berry," said Starkey. "That what you mean?"

Slocum nodded. "And I'd bet that he'll back him all the way," he said. "Almost for sure, he's on Berry's payroll."

"We can't count on the law," said Starkey.

"I never knew a time when you could," Slocum added. "You got to take care of your own troubles."

"Well, hell," said Starkey, "let's go on down to the store and get loaded up."

The general store was owned and run by a man named Chilly Kirkpatrick. Starkey introduced Slocum and left a list with Kirkpatrick. "I'll meet you back at the ranch later," he said to Slocum, and he went out the front door, leaving Slocum to deal with the supplies.

"I ain't seen you before. Reckon you just started with Sam," said Chilly.

"Yesterday morning," said Slocum.

"He's a good boy," said Chilly. "I knowed his daddy. Yeah. He's a pretty good boy, but I'm afraid he's making a fool play, and you are, too, if you're planning to stick with him."

"How's that?" Slocum asked.

"You don't know?"

"You making reference to a man called Berry?" said Slocum.

Chilly, stacking supplies on the counter, nodded his head. "You know," he said. "Then you ought to know that it's a fool play, and you ought to be old enough to know why."

"Yeah," said Slocum. "You're right. I do know. In fact, when I first found out about it, I made up my mind to just move on and leave the young fool to fight his own fight."

"Why didn't you?"

"Your damn sheriff told me to get out of town," Slocum said.

"Pride's killed many a man," Chilly muttered. "It'll kill more."

"Yeah," said Slocum. "Well, why don't you just tally this stuff up and let me get the hell out of here?"

"Meaning keep my mouth shut?"

"You said it. Not me. Say," said Slocum. "It just occurred to me that you're making a pretty damn fool move here yourself."

"Yeah? What's that?"

"You putting all this stuff on the tab? I didn't see Starkey pay for it, and I damn sure ain't paying."

"Sam's got credit," said Chilly.

"And if he gets himself killed," Slocum asked, "then who pays?"

"You're right," said Chilly. "I'm another fool around here. That don't mean I can't point out foolishness to others, does it? What do you think'll happen to me once Berry's got his hands on all the land in the valley? You think he'll want to stop there? Once he gets his mind free, he'll start looking around for what else he can grab, and I do a pretty good business here. What do you think'll happen to me then? Huh?''

"I reckon you might be a target," said Slocum. "In fact, I don't imagine that Berry'd be any too pleased to know that you're helping Starkey hang on by giving him credit."

"What Berry don't know won't hurt him," Chilly said. Then he looked up at Slocum with a little grin on his face, and he winked. "Or maybe it will."

Chilly finished his tally, then helped Slocum load the wagon. They were just about finished, and Slocum was carrying the last bag of flour out, when he nearly ran into a young woman coming into the store. He backed up.

"Excuse me, ma'am," he said.

"Slocum, isn't it?" she said.

Slocum looked up and recognized Brandy Berry. With his free hand he touched the brim of his hat. "Oh," he said, "sorry. I wasn't looking, Miss Berry." He moved on through the door and down to the wagon. Brandy followed him out onto the boardwalk.

"Obviously," she said.

Slocum flung the flour sack onto the load and turned to look at her. "I apologized twice," he said. "Ain't that enough for you?"

"Yes," she said. "I guess it is. I'm just surprised to see you still here. That's all."

"Why wouldn't I still be here?" Slocum asked her. "I've got a job."

"I figured that maybe you'd heard by now about the situation Sam's got himself in here in the valley," Brandy said. "And I figured that a man like you would just move on when he knew there was trouble coming.''

''What do you mean by a man like me?'' he asked.

''A man who won't jump into a fight,'' she said.

''I already told you my thinking on that,'' he said. ''If you can't understand it, there ain't no reason going into it again.''

''I remember what you said.''

''Maybe you'll answer a question for me,'' Slocum said.

''Maybe.''

''What're you doing messing with Starkey anyhow? Your daddy's trying to buy him out and threatening to run him out if he won't sell.''

''My daddy's business is his business,'' said Brandy. ''No one can tell him what to do. And my business is my business. No one tells me what to do either. Does that satisfy your curiosity, Mr. Slocum?''

''For the time being,'' he said. He gave a polite tug to the front of his hat brim, walked to the front of the wagon, and climbed up onto the seat.

''Mr. Slocum,'' Brandy said.

He looked back over his shoulder. ''Yes, ma'am?''

''I'm—very fond of Sam Starkey,'' she said.

''You kind of showed that the first time I saw you,'' he said.

''If my father runs Sam out of the valley, I'll go with Sam.''

''Have you told him that?'' Slocum asked. ''Or have you told your daddy?'' She didn't answer. ''Well, that's real nice, Miss Berry,'' said Slocum. ''What'll you do if your daddy kills Sam? Sing at the funeral?''

5

Slocum was pumping water from a well in front of the house. Smoke was rising from the chimney behind him, for Sam Starkey was inside, cooking breakfast. When the bucket was about full, Slocum stopped pumping, straightened up, and then noticed some riders coming down the lane toward the house, six of them. He picked up the bucket and went back inside. The smell of bacon frying and coffee boiling filled his nostrils.

"Thanks, Slocum," said Starkey as Slocum set the bucket down.

"Riders coming," said Slocum.

"How many?"

"Six."

Starkey grabbed his gun belt and strapped it on.

37

Then he hurried over to the nearest front window to look out. "It's Berry and some of his hands," he said. "You stay inside." He moved to the front door, opened it, and stepped outside onto the porch to wait for his uninvited guests. Slocum crossed the room to the window on the other side of the door, picking up his Winchester along the way. He cranked a shell into the chamber and pressed his back against the wall beside the window.

Outside, the six riders came close to the house and stopped. Their horses stirred up a dust cloud that blew across the front of the house. Starkey squinted through it at Berry. To Berry's immediate right rode Jo Jo. Homer Drink was on his left, and there were three other Berry hands with them. All of them were armed with six-guns and rifles, and all their faces were set hard—all except Berry's. The big rancher touched the brim of his hat and smiled at Sam Starkey.

" 'Morning, Sam," he said. He was a stout man with a slight middle-age paunch which did not, however, seem to indicate any developing softness. He dressed like a working rancher, not like a man who let others do all of his work. A heavy mustache drooped over his upper lip. Starkey stood silent. "Mind if we step down and set a spell?" Berry asked.

"I mind," said Starkey.

"That ain't very neighborly," said Jo Jo through a scowl.

"I ain't feeling neighborly," Starkey said. "Not to you. Not now and not anytime."

"I heard about that little fight you and Jo Jo had the other day," said Berry. "That was personal between the two of you. I had nothing to do with it. If I was to send him on back home, would you be inclined to be more friendly then?''

"I doubt it," said Starkey. "Why don't you just say what it is you came over here to say and then get the hell on out of here?''

"Now, say, I came over here for a friendly chat," said Berry.

"With five armed men backing you up?''

"Aw, hell, that don't mean nothing," said Berry. "Hell, you never know who you might meet out on the road these days. It pays to be careful. That's all. But I'll send them all back to the ranch anyhow and sit down with you, just you and me. How's that?''

"It wouldn't make any difference, Berry," Starkey said. "You and me got nothing to talk about.''

"I think we have," said Berry, leaning forward in his saddle. "You got a nice little ranch here, son, but you got no future with it. You got no cows on the place. You got no crew to work the place, and I happen to know that you got no money in the bank.''

"That's none of your damn business," said Starkey. "That's just between me and the bank.''

Berry grinned. "But I happen to know it all anyhow," he said. "Whatever you try to do out here, you're going to be competing against me, and you got no chance of coming out ahead. Hell, even if you was to get some more cattle, I can undersell you easy. Cut you right out of the market. Nothing personal in it. It's just business. That's all. Now, I'm trying to help you out here, Sam. I don't want to see you go under that way.''

"You're trying to run me off," said Starkey. "That's what you're trying to do. You've done it to everyone else in the valley, and now you're after me. Well, by God, it ain't going to work with me. This is my home, and I'm sticking."

"That ain't no nice way to talk," said Jo Jo, his horse fidgeting under him. His right hand rested not so casually on the butt of his revolver.

"Shut up, Jo Jo," said Berry. "I'm talking here. Sam, pay no mind to what he said. I just don't want to see you lose everything. If you try to hang on here, that's just what's going to happen. You'll lose everything and ride out of this valley broke. Now, I've made you a fair and honest offer for your place. Why don't you take it?"

"I told you before," said Starkey. "I don't want to sell. This is my home, and I like it here. I ain't leaving this valley."

"Oh, you'll leave it all right," said Berry. "One way or the other."

"Leave it now with some bucks in your jeans," said Jo Jo, "or leave it later dead broke. Or maybe just dead." A snide grin rode up on one side of Jo Jo's face.

"That's just the kind of threat I was waiting to hear," said Starkey. "Now, get off my land. All of you."

"Sam," said Berry.

"Get out of here now," said Starkey.

"We'll see about that," said Jo Jo, starting to haul out his six-gun.

"I wouldn't do that if I was you," said Slocum,

and all of the Berry crew looked toward the ominous voice that had just surprised them. They saw the gleaming barrel of Slocum's Winchester leveled at them through the open window. Starkey took advantage of their momentary distraction to pull his own revolver out and thumb back the hammer. He pointed the barrel directly at Ben Berry's thick chest.

Berry took in the situation real quick. "Jo Jo," he snapped, "cut it out. We didn't come here to make any trouble. We came to talk. Come on now. Let's get out of here."

The Berry riders turned their mounts to head back out to the road. But Berry himself looked back over his shoulder for one last comment to Starkey as he rode away. "I still hope you'll change your mind," he said in a loud voice. "Come on over to see me when you've come to your senses."

Starkey stood on the porch until the riders had gotten well away from the house. Then he turned and went back inside. He stepped quickly over to the stove.

"Goddammit," he said. "I've burned up the damn bacon."

Slocum put down his Winchester and walked over to look in the pan. "Aw," he said. "That ain't bad. I've ate a lot worse than that."

Starkey scooped out the bacon and tossed it on a platter. Then he sliced some more and put it in the skillet. He broke some eggs in another pan and started to scramble them. Slocum sniffed at the coffee boiling on the back of the stove.

"This here's done," he said. "Want me to pour you a cup?"

"Yeah. Thanks."

Slocum poured coffee into two cups and set one down within Starkey's reach. Then he sat at the table and took a tentative sip from his cup.

"Damn," he said. "It's hot."

"Hell, it's been on the fire," said Starkey.

"Yeah." Slocum leaned back in his chair. "That Jo Jo fella," he said, "acts like he wants to be a ramrod real bad."

"You mean he's wanting to take over my ranch?" Starkey asked. He scooped the eggs out onto the platter and set the platter down on the table in front of Slocum. Slocum scraped some of the eggs and most of the burnt bacon out onto a plate. He reached for a biscuit from a bowlful that had been sitting on the table, waiting for the bacon and eggs to be ready.

"Well," he said, "he wants that too, but I mean, he seems like he wants to take over every damn thing. Take over the whole operation from his own boss."

"He's a pushy little shit," said Starkey. "I'm surprised that Berry let him get away with talking like that."

"It's strategy," said Slocum. "Berry talks nice to you, pretending to be on the up-and-up, but he has Jo Jo to make sure you know what's likely to happen if you don't cooperate." He forked some eggs with one hand and picked up a slice of his very crisp bacon with the other. "He's even after your girl," he said.

Starkey turned away from the stove to face Slocum. "You know," he said, "I think it's all part of the same dirty game. I think the weasly little son of a bitch wants to help his boss get my ranch. Then I think he wants to marry Brandy, and then get rid of old Berry some way. Then he'd have it all. All for himself. That's what I think he wants.''

Slocum swallowed. ''Could be,'' he said. He picked up his cup for a slurp of coffee. ''It's not a bad scheme either.''

''But it'll never work,'' said Starkey, turning back to tend the bacon.

''Why not?'' asked Slocum, shoveling in another mouthful.

''In the first place,'' Starkey said, ''they ain't getting rid of me so easy. In the second place, Brandy won't have anything to do with Jo Jo. Hell, she can't hardly stand the sight of him.''

''Maybe,'' said Slocum. ''Then again, Jo Jo's ambitions just might work to our advantage.''

Starkey was scooping out the bacon onto the platter. ''How's that?'' he asked.

''I don't know just yet,'' said Slocum. ''But it might if we just wait and watch for the right opportunity. Tell me about that Berry.''

''What do you want to know?'' asked Starkey, sitting down at the table.

''Whatever you know about him. How long has he been around these parts?''

''Oh, long as I can remember,'' Starkey said. ''He used to be all right too. Just a hardworking rancher. He seemed to struggle along pretty much like the rest of us. That was when my folks were still around, and I was just a kid. When I lost my folks, I wound up here alone with the ranch. Things were all right for a couple of years. Then Berry lost his wife. It was just a couple of months after that, I guess, that he started to change.''

"All because his wife died?" Slocum asked.

"I don't know," Starkey continued. "That must have been part of it. It seemed to turn him kind of hard and mean. And then Brandy was only just about fourteen, and she got kind of ornery. The old man was trying to raise her without a mother. That must have been hard on him too. Anyhow, financially he was just getting to be in pretty good shape when that happened. All those years of hard work had started to pay off, and then that old Gulley up at the far end of the valley decided he wanted to sell out. Well, Berry bought Gulley's place, and that started it. He just seemed to want to keep on buying and buy up the whole damn valley.''

"Could be that meanness was in him all along," said Slocum. "Two things let it out. His wife might have been what was keeping him in line, and then, too, he hadn't had the money before to make his move with.''

"Yeah," said Starkey, "that makes sense. I hadn't thought about it quite like that before, but it does make sense.''

" 'Course," said Slocum, "it don't really matter much one way or the other. What matters is what he's doing and how to stop him from doing it.''

"Yeah," said Starkey.

Both men were through eating, but they each got another cup of coffee and continued to sit at the table and talk. It might not make the job any easier knowing why Berry was doing what he was doing, but it was something to talk about, and it satisfied the curiosity.

"What about that Jo Jo?" Slocum asked. "How long has he been with Berry?"

"Right after Berry got hold of Gulley's place and started in with his land grabbing," said Starkey, "he found that weasel somewhere and hired him on. He's been around only a couple of years. No one seems to know where the hell he came from. I think old Berry just rolled over a big rock and Jo Jo come crawling out."

"Well, he's the one to watch out for," said Slocum. "I've seen his kind before."

They finished their coffee, and then together they washed, dried, and put away the dishes. Outside on the porch, Slocum lit a cigar. He offered one to Starkey, but Starkey politely turned it down. Slocum leaned back against a post and puffed.

"Boss," he said, "you know these men a hell of a lot better than I do. What do you think they'll pull next?"

"One of two things," said Starkey. "They could just sit back and wait for me to go broke and come crawling to Berry to buy me out. They could, but I don't think they will. I don't think that Berry's got the patience for that, and I know that Jo Jo ain't."

"So what will they do?"

"Berry won't come around with no more offers," Starkey said. "When they come back it'll be with guns or torches or both, and it'll likely be at night. And Berry won't be with them for that kind of work.

When they pull something, he'll deny that he had anything to do with it, and that worthless sheriff in Dead
Dog will back him up all the way.''

"How soon, do you think?" Slocum asked.

"Anytime now," said Starkey. "Anytime. That's
my best guess. You want to pull out?"

"No," said Slocum. "Hell, I ought to, but I ain't
going to. No one ever did accuse me of having much
good sense. But I do think we ought to get ready for
them, if you think that's what they're fixing to do. I
don't much like the idea of being sneaked up on and
caught with my pants down."

"No," said Starkey. "Me neither."

6

As Slocum was the entire crew of the SS Ranch, Sam Starkey had put an extra bed in the main and only house for Slocum to sleep in. They'd had another lazy day at the ranch, with no word about the expected herd of cattle, and after a big meal they turned in early.

Slocum was drifting off to sleep with thoughts about Veronica swimming in his head and stirring his loins. He was thinking that except for the pay he was getting from Starkey for doing next to nothing, he'd have been better off to stay in Dead Dog and drink and gamble and whore around. He'd have been better off except for one thing. Without his do-nothing job here at the SS, he wouldn't have any money with which to do those things. Of course, Veronica had said

47

that his money was no good in her place, but then, that couldn't last forever either.

Across the room Starkey was already asleep. Slocum could tell by the heavy, rhythmic breathing. He could also tell that he himself was on the verge of dropping off, for he was no longer sure whether his thoughts were conscious thoughts or fragments of dreams. He imagined that he could hear the sounds of approaching horses. They were not riding hard. They were approaching at a leisurely pace. They were quiet. They were trying to be quiet, almost as if they were trying to come upon someone in secret so as to take them by surprise.

Those thoughts forced Slocum to open his eyes and try to wake up. Was it a dream, imagination, or reality? Riders coming? Coming quietly in the night? He threw back his blanket and sat up on the edge of the bed. He walked barefoot across the room to where his Winchester leaned against the wall, picked up the rifle, and moved to one of the front windows. He leaned against the wall beside the window and cautiously peered outside.

It was a dark night. Still, he could make out the silhouettes of at least six riders. He hurried over to Starkey's bed and gave his boss a quick shake. Starkey raised his groggy head and rubbed his bleary eyes with the back of a hand.

"Huh?" he muttered. "What? What is it, Slocum?"

"Get up, boss," said Slocum. "We got visitors."

Starkey woke up fast. By the time he got his hands on his own rifle, Slocum was already back at the window. Starkey moved quickly to the other window and looked out. The rider in the middle of the group outside seemed to be giving last-minute instructions. His voice was low, but now and then it carried into the house. No understandable words came through though, only a muttering sound. But his gestures were clear.

Then the riders began to move slowly, spreading out to the sides in both directions. One struck a match, and before either of the men inside could react, he touched it to a torch that flared up instantly in the darkness. Starkey flung up the window and poked the barrel of his rifle out. Slocum did the same.

"Hold it right there," Starkey called.

"Toss it," called a voice from outside, and the man with the torch swung his arm and let the torch fly. It banged against the front door and fell to the porch. Starkey squeezed his trigger, and the torch thrower clutched at his shoulder and slumped in his saddle. Slocum fired, and another rider slumped.

"Scatter," called the voice from outside.

Slocum fired again and so did Starkey, but the targets were moving and disappearing in the darkness. Some of them fired back, and the glass in the window by Slocum was shattered. He threw himself back against the wall to avoid the flying and falling shards. He thought about the glass on the floor, and he wished that he had taken the time to pull on his boots when he first got out of bed.

"Are you hit?" Starkey asked.

"No," said Slocum. "I'm all right. I'm just standing barefoot in a pile of glass. That's all."

"Well, hell, don't move," said Starkey.

"I ain't."

It was suddenly quiet. There were no more shots, no more shouted orders from outside. The silence was eerie and in a strange way disturbing.

"What the hell are they doing out there?" Starkey said in a harsh whisper.

"I don't know," said Slocum, "but I think I hear wood burning. I smell it too."

Starkey ran over to his bed, sat down, and pulled on his boots. Then he hurried over to Slocum's bed and picked up Slocum's boots. He raced across the room and handed the boots to Slocum.

"Here," he said. "Get your boots on."

Slocum leaned his rifle against the wall and lifted one foot to pull on a boot. Starkey moved to the doorway. Smoke was coming in under the door. Slocum pulled on his other boot.

"The damn porch is on fire," said Starkey. He opened the door, and the bright flames almost blinded him. They were already up to the doorway. A shot was fired from somewhere out in the darkness, and the bullet thudded into the door frame just to the right of Starkey's head.

"Damn," he said, jumping back and slamming the door. "What the hell're we going to do? The goddamn house will be on fire in a minute."

"Go out the back door," said Slocum. "Go around the house and shoot any goddamn thing we see."

"Let's go, then," said Starkey.

He reached the back door first and jerked it open. Stepping out, he turned to his left. "You go the other way," he said. Slocum turned right. Staying close to the house, he moved quickly to the corner, stopped, and looked around.

He saw a rider there, out in front and to the side of the house. The man was just sitting there on his horse, a six-gun in his hand. He must have been watching the front door for someone to try to come out again to fight the fire. Slocum raised his rifle to his shoulder, aimed quickly, and snapped off a shot.

The man jerked in the saddle and screamed, but he kept his seat, kicked his horse in the sides, and started to ride. Letting the man go, Slocum moved along the side of the house toward the front corner. He heard two shots and figured that Starkey had found a target or two on the other side of the house. He looked around the corner for someone else to shoot at, just as the leader of the gang shouted another order.

"Let's get the hell out of here."

Horses' hooves began to pound. The wind blew the smoke from the fire on the porch across Slocum's line of sight. He heard two more shots. Starkey's? Boldly he ran through the drifting smoke just in time to see the riders escaping down the lane that led off the ranch to the main road. He raised his rifle and fired a couple of shots after them.

"Starkey?" he called. "Hey, boss. You all right?"

Starkey stepped out from behind the far corner of the house.

"Yeah, I'm all right," he said, "but the bastards tore down the fence. The horses are out."

"The horses will have to wait," said Slocum. "We'd best get that fire out quick."

Slocum stroked the pump handle while Starkey ran with a bucket. They soon had the fire out, but the porch was ruined, and so was the front door. The door frame was partially burned too, and it would have to be replaced. The house was filled with smoke, and, of course, one front window was broken. With the fire out, they turned their attention to the loose horses.

Slocum's big 'Palouse was the first one they found. It hadn't wandered far and was easy for Slocum to catch. Starkey got hold of another. They led the two horses back into the corral and started picking up fence rails and lifting them back into place.

"Well," said Starkey, "that'll have to do for now. We'll do a better job of it come daylight."

"What about the other horses?" Slocum asked.

"We'd never find them in the dark," said Starkey. "They'll have to wait for daylight too. Damn. That son of a bitch."

"Berry?"

"Who else? I knew it was coming, but I didn't think it would be this soon or this sudden. Goddammit."

"Well, boss," said Slocum, "look on the bright side."

"Yeah?" said Starkey. "You find a bright side to all this?"

"You got some real work for me to do now," said Slocum. "Hell, we got horses to catch, a fence to mend, and a house to repair. And right now one of us ought to stay awake and keep watch, and it might as well be me, 'cause I'm damn sure wide awake."

"Yeah," said Starkey. "We'll have to sleep in

shifts from now on, I guess. You going to get your britches on, or you going to stand out here in your longjohns?''

"It don't make a hell of a lot of difference," said Slocum. "No one's going to see me out here in the dark."

"Not unless some of Berry's men come back," said Starkey.

"I don't really expect them again tonight," said Slocum, "but if they do come back, I'll see them first this time."

"Come on in the house," said Starkey. "They ain't coming back right away, and if you're going to stay up awhile, I'll make you some fresh coffee."

"Sounds good," said Slocum, and he followed Starkey back into the house. Starkey lit a lamp, then stoked up the fire in the stove. He put some coffee on to boil, then sat down heavily in a chair at the table.

"I don't think they'll come back tonight at all, Slocum," he said. "I know we hit a couple of them."

"I got two of them for sure," said Slocum.

"I know I hit one. Maybe two."

"Then I'd say we hurt them pretty bad," said Slocum. "That's four out of the six."

"Yeah," said Starkey, "but like you say, there was only six of them here. Berry's got twenty cowhands or more. Over all, we didn't hurt him too bad. He's still got us way outnumbered."

"Well," said Slocum, "like you say, they probably won't be back tonight, but I still think I'll go on out and watch."

He started moving toward the door.

"I'll fetch you a cup when the coffee's done," Starkey said.

"Thanks."

Slocum went outside. The porch was caved in in the center, where it had burned. There was no great damage done. They still had a house to sleep in, a place to get in out of the weather, and if they managed to round up all the horses in the morning, the worst of it all was that they would have some patching-up work to do. Mainly it was annoying.

Their sleep had been disturbed. A nice little house had been marred, and it would take some time and expense to repair it. The fence would take only time and a little sweat to fix up. They would probably be able to round up all the horses.

It was the idea of what had happened that so angered Slocum. It was an extension of Dancer's having told Slocum to get out of town. This was the same order issued a bit more forcefully, and Slocum liked it even less than he had the first time, when it had come from the sheriff's fat lips. It was Starkey's ranch, Starkey's home, but Slocum by now felt as if he had almost as much stake in it as had the owner.

It wasn't the land, and it wasn't the living that could come from the land. It certainly wasn't the idea of home that went with land. But it was something just as significant to Slocum. It was pride and freedom and his ideas about right and wrong. If someone's minding his own business, no one else has got the right to tell him to pack up and get out. And with Slocum it was one of the fastest ways to convince him to stick—no matter what.

•   •   •

They spent the next day catching horses and fixing the corral, and by midafternoon it was all done. The fence was as good as ever, and all the horses were back inside. For the rest of the working day they pulled the burned boards off the porch and tossed them in a pile well away from the house. The door frame and door would have to stay as they were until new ones had been built.

Starkey showed Slocum where he had a pile of lumber in the barn, and they started cutting boards to rebuild the porch and the door frame. When the sun went down, they quit working and had their supper. Starkey went to bed. Slocum stood the first watch again.

7

After a hearty breakfast the next morning Slocum was prepared to resume his work as a carpenter, but Starkey surprised him when he started to hitch up the wagon and said, "Saddle me a horse, Slocum."

"Where we going?" Slocum asked.

"We're going into town," said Starkey.

When the wagon and the saddle horse were ready, Starkey climbed onto the back of the horse and gestured toward the wagon. "You drive," he said.

Slocum climbed onto the seat and gathered up the reins. "What're we up to, boss?" he asked.

"First we're going to pick us up a new door and some window glass from old Chilly," said Starkey, "and then we're going to stop by the sheriff's office and report what happened out here the other night."

Starkey had already started riding, and Slocum snapped the reins. The wagon moved forward with a jerk.

"You reckon that'll do any good?" he asked.

"Nope," said Starkey, "but it's got to be reported anyhow."

"Don't see why," said Slocum, muttering to himself.

They didn't talk much the rest of the way into Dead Dog, but Slocum kept asking himself why the hell Starkey wanted to bother with that damn worthless Dancer. Any talk to that sorry excuse for a lawman would be wasted time and wasted effort. But Starkey was the boss, so Slocum kept his opinion to himself. He'd ride along and do what he was told—up to a point.

When they reached town and pulled up in front of Dancer's office, Starkey dismounted and hitched his horse to the rail. "Come on," he said. Slocum heaved a sigh and set the brake on the wagon. He climbed down and followed Starkey into the office, where they found the sheriff as before, sitting behind his desk and looking as if he'd been there for several days. Dancer looked up and snarled when he saw who his visitors were.

"You two," he said. "What the hell do you want this time?"

"Dancer," said Starkey, "night before last, six men rode out in the dark and attacked me in my home. They fired shots into my house, broke a window, and tried to kill me and Slocum here. They set fire to my porch and would have burned the house down if we hadn't managed to run them off and put the fire out.''

"Who were they?" Dancer asked.

"I know who they were," said Starkey, "and so do you, but we couldn't see any of them clearly. Like I said, it was dark.''

"Ain't nothing I can do if you can't identify any of them," said Dancer. "You know that. We've been through it all before.''

"And you know as well as I do who it is that wants me out of this valley," Starkey said. "You could at least take a ride out there and question him and some of his boys.''

"You reckon they going to just own up to it if I was to do that?" said the sheriff. "Now, that would surely be an amazing thing. Just be a hell of a waste of time. That's all.''

"Just like coming here to tell you about what happened," said Slocum. "Right?''

"Now, just what the hell is that supposed to mean?" Starkey asked, frowning at Slocum.

"Take it any way you want, Sheriff," Slocum said.

"I'll tell you how I take it," said Dancer, coming to his feet. "You say that you was attacked at night by six men who shot at you and set your house on fire. You ain't either one of you hurt, and you managed to drive them off and save your house.''

"Well, that's the way it happened," Starkey said.

"We clipped four of them," said Slocum. "Be interesting to see if any of Berry's cowhands have got broken wings.''

"I ain't seen no wounded cowhands," said Dancer,

"and I ain't had no complaints about shot cowhands. I ain't going to insult Mr. Berry by telling him this tale, and I don't want to hear no more complaints from either one of you jaspers unless you bring in some proof of what you're talking about. You got that?"

Slocum turned and headed for the door. "Let's go, boss," he said.

"I got it," said Starkey, "but I'm here to tell you that Berry has started a war with that raid on my house, and whatever happens next, I just want to make damn sure that you know who it was that started the shooting. It wasn't me that fired the first shot. That's all."

Starkey followed Slocum out the door and headed for his horse. Slocum moved back to the wagon.

"Well," said Starkey, "you were right about that. Still, I feel better having told him about it. Let's go down to Chilly's store."

The door of Dancer's office came open, and the sheriff's massive figure filled the doorway. He leaned out as he called to Starkey. "Listen, boy, don't you go starting no trouble with Mr. Berry. You do that, and I'll have to come after you."

"The trouble's already been started," said Slocum.

"You'd like that, wouldn't you?" Starkey said.

"Like what?" said Dancer.

"An excuse to come after me."

"I got a question for you, Sheriff," said Slocum.

"What's that?" Dancer asked.

"How much is Berry paying you?"

"Ah, get out of here," said the sheriff. He backed into his office and slammed the door.

Starkey started riding toward the store, and Slocum climbed up onto the wagon seat. He released the brake, gathered up the reins, and followed Starkey. They pulled up again, this time in front of Chilly Kirkpatrick's general store, and Slocum followed Starkey inside.

"Howdy, boys," said Kirkpatrick. "What can I do for you today?"

"Howdy, Chilly," said Starkey. "I need a new front door for my house."

"You just put one on not long ago," said Kirkpatrick. "Something wrong with it?"

"It was just fine until night before last, when some night riders came out for a visit," said Starkey. "They tried to burn me out."

"Damn," said Kirkpatrick. "Well, hell, I knew it was coming though. Told you so too, didn't I?"

"You did," said Starkey. "More than once."

"What happened?"

"I told you."

"All you said was that some night riders tried to burn you out," said Kirkpatrick. "That's all you said. I know damn well there's more to it than that. Tell me the rest."

"Well," said Starkey, "they shot the house up pretty good, and they tossed a torch on the front steps to start the fire. Me and Slocum managed to drive them off after we winged three or four of them, and then we got the fire out. Oh, yeah. They tore down the corral and turned the horses out, but we got them all back and repaired the fence okay."

"Damn," said Kirkpatrick. Then, lowering his

voice, he said, "I seen Homer Drink this morning. He had his arm in a sling. He said he fell off his horse."

"I bet he did," said Slocum, "after a bullet hit him."

"You got that door?" Starkey asked. "Oh, yeah. I need a window glass too."

They loaded the door and the glass into the wagon, and Starkey told Slocum to drive it back to the ranch. "I'll see you out there in a while," he said.

Slocum thought that it probably wasn't a good idea for either one of them to be riding around alone, but then, Starkey was the boss. For himself, he'd just keep his eyes open and be ready for anything or anybody. He hoped that Starkey would be able to take care of himself. He shook his head, flicked the reins, and headed for the SS, wondering again just why the hell he was mixed up in this damn fool business.

Starkey rode up to the big main house on Berry's ranch. As he came close, two cowhands rode up, one on either side of him. Neither said a word. They just continued alongside him as he moved closer to the house. Then he saw Jo Jo Darby standing on the porch, his arms folded across his chest. Starkey halted his mount a few feet away from the porch. The two Berry riders remained mounted on each side of him. If he had wanted to dismount, he barely had room to do so.

"What the hell do you want here, Starkey?" Jo Jo said.

"I came out to have a talk with your boss," said

Starkey. "I sure as hell don't want to talk to you. You want to tell him I'm here?"

"You ready to sell out, are you?" asked Jo Jo. "Had enough?"

"Enough of what?" Starkey asked. "Are you admitting that you attacked my house?"

"I ain't admitting nothing," said Jo Jo. "Just asked if you was ready to sell out. That's all."

"I told you," said Starkey, "I came to talk to Berry, not to you."

"Well," said Jo Jo, "Mr. Berry ain't got nothing to talk to you about, not unless you want to talk about selling, and, uh, by the way, the offer's gone down somewhat since last he made it. You should have took it then."

"You going to tell Berry I'm here?" Starkey asked.

"I done told you how it is," said Jo Jo.

"I guess I'll have to tell him myself," said Starkey. He started to swing down out of the saddle, but the rider to his left edged even closer. "You're crowding me," said Starkey.

"Help him down, boys," said Jo Jo.

The rider to Starkey's right suddenly reached over and grabbed a handful of Starkey's shirt. He yelled and kicked his horse, causing it to lurch to the right. Starkey was dragged from the saddle and dropped hard on the ground. The unexpected jolt knocked all the wind from his lungs, and for a moment all he could do was raise his arms to shield himself from the stamping hooves of his own surprised and fidgeting horse.

Both Berry riders quickly dismounted and ran to

the fallen Starkey. They reached down and grabbed an arm each, then pulled him to his feet and held him up. Starkey was still gasping for breath, and he hung limply between the two cowboys. Jo Jo walked slowly down from the porch and over to stand in front of the helpless Starkey. He slipped a pair of gloves out of his hip pocket and pulled them on.

"It was pretty dumb of you to ride over here all by yourself," he said. "Pretty damn stupid." He drove a fist into Starkey's gut, and Starkey's gasps for breath grew even more desperate. Jo Jo laughed a little and hit Starkey again, the same way. "Maybe now you're ready to sell out," Jo Jo said. Starkey sucked wind. "No?" said Jo Jo. He drove another fist into Starkey's midsection, and what little air Starkey had managed to suck in was driven out again in a loud whoosh.

"I don't think he can talk, Jo Jo," said one of the cowboys.

"I don't think he wants to," said Jo Jo. "He don't yet think that I mean business here. I been too damn easy on him."

Jo Jo reached out, took a handful of Starkey's hair, and jerked Starkey's head up and back, then he swung a right and bashed the side of Starkey's head. Starkey saw stars. Jo Jo took another swing and hit the other side. Starkey thought that it couldn't last much longer. Another punch or two like that, and he would pass out.

He was vaguely aware of the sound of a screen door slamming somewhere in the background, and then, as if through a tunnel from a long distance, he heard the familiar voice of Brandy Berry.

"Stop it," she said. "Jo Jo. Stop that right now."

"Miss Berry," said Jo Jo. "This here is men's business. You just go on back in the house."

"What you're doing has nothing to do with business," said Brandy. "Let him go."

The two cowboys looked at Jo Jo.

"Just hold on to him, boys," Jo Jo said. "Hell, sweetie, if they let go of him, he'll just fall down. Now, why don't you just take your pretty little butt on back in the house and let me handle this?"

Starkey was taking full advantage of the lull in the activities to draw some breath back into his lungs. He still allowed his full weight to hang on the two cowboys though. Perhaps it would keep them off guard. They didn't need to know yet that he was making any kind of recovery.

Brandy came down from the porch and walked toward Jo Jo. "I said, let him go," she demanded, "and I mean it."

Jo Jo turned toward her, exasperated. He held his arms out to his sides, and his legs were spread wide. "Dammit, Brandy," he said, but he didn't get any further with his speech. Starkey straightened himself up and delivered a hard and swift kick that went right up between Jo Jo's legs. It would have been a kick in the ass, but the toe of Starkey's boot lapped around to whop Jo Jo's balls.

The kick made a loud slapping sound, and Jo Jo roared in pain, doubled over, grabbing at his crotch, and dropped to his knees. His eyes opened wide and his face turned green. The cowboys looked at each other, wondering what to do. Brandy walked right past the groveling Jo Jo, who was sounding as if he might puke just anytime now. She stepped up to face the other two, still holding Starkey's arms.

"Let him go," she said. They did, and Starkey managed to hold himself up on his own legs. "Now, get on out of here," Brandy said to the cowboys, "and take him with you." She nodded over her shoulder toward the retching Jo Jo. The cowboys moved quickly to Jo Jo's aid, but he wasn't nearly ready to be helped up to his feet. Brandy looked at Starkey. "Are you okay?" she asked.

"I'll mend," Starkey said. "Thanks."

"I'm sorry that happened," she said. "I'll talk to Dad about it."

"Don't bother," said Starkey. He looked around for his hat. Finding it a few feet away, he walked over to pick it up, batted it against his leg a couple of times to knock off the dust, then put it on. "I'll be going," he said, and he walked toward his horse. Brandy followed him.

"Sammy," she said, "Dad didn't have anything to do with this."

"I notice he didn't come out to stop it," said Starkey. He caught his horse by the reins and moved to its side to mount. "I came over here just to have a talk with him," he continued. "You saw the reception I got." He swung up onto the back of his horse.

"Wait, Sammy," said Brandy, but Starkey was already on his way back toward the main road. "Sammy," she called. He kept going. Brandy turned and stomped back to the house. Coming back alongside Jo Jo, who was still on his knees and still moaning, she paused. "You couldn't whip him by yourself," she snapped, "so you got these two to help you." She strode back up onto the porch, jerked open the door, and went back into the house, slamming the door behind herself. Jo Jo raised his head a little and looked after her.

"I'll kill that goddamned Starkey," he said. He panted heavily a few times, then added, "and I'll get her too."

Back out on the road, Starkey moved slowly. Even the steady and easy rolling of the walking horse beneath him caused the pains from his beating to shoot through his body. Now and then he groaned out loud. He had aimed his horse back toward the SS. There would be no point in making a special trip into town to report this latest episode to Sheriff Dancer.

Dancer wouldn't do a damn thing about it. In fact, if past experience proved anything, Starkey thought, Dancer would be much more likely to accuse him of having gone over to Berry's ranch deliberately to start the fight in the first place. He moaned out loud, partly from the pain and partly from thinking about Dancer's attitude. Slocum had been right about the crooked sheriff from the beginning.

Starkey was eager to get back to his ranch and crawl into his bed after a quick washing-up. Then he thought again about Slocum, and he moaned again. Slocum had warned him, and Starkey didn't relish listening to Slocum saying I told you so. He might not actually say anything, but it would show on his face. It would be clear enough what he was thinking. If he wasn't hurting so badly, he thought, he just wouldn't go home for a while. But nothing else made any sense under the circumstances, so he kept on his way. He would just have to put up with it, and, he grudgingly admitted to himself, he probably deserved every bit of it. Seemed like that damned Slocum was always right.

8

From where he was fitting the new door, Slocum looked over his shoulder to see Starkey riding up the lane toward the house. As soon as he knew the approaching rider was friendly, he resumed his work. In a moment he glanced over his shoulder again. This time Starkey was nearly up to the porch, and Slocum could see at a glance that his boss had been beaten again. He turned around to face Starkey and heaved a long, exasperated sigh.

"Shit," he said. "Not again."

"Shut up, Slocum," said Starkey. He groaned as he started to get off his horse. Slocum moved down off the porch to give him a hand.

"I knew goddamn well I shouldn't have let you ride off by yourself," he said, "but no one can tell you anything, can they? You got to just keep on learning things the hard way."

"I said shut up," Starkey said. He was standing on his own feet by this time, and he took his horse by the reins. Slocum took them away from him.

"I'll take care of him," he said. "You just get on in the house and take care of yourself."

"Who the hell's the boss around here anyhow?" said Starkey.

"The boss ain't got as much sense as this damn horse," said Slocum, leading the animal toward the corral. Starkey started to snap back something but groaned instead, then turned to go into the house. By the time Slocum got back from the corral, Starkey was lying on his cot, moaning. Slocum stood just inside the door, hands on hips, staring at Starkey.

"What?" said Starkey. "Well, what the hell is it? What do you want to say?"

"I done said what I had to say," said Slocum. "You got anything you want to tell me about?"

"No."

"You got me right square in the middle of your damn fix," said Slocum. "I reckon you'd best tell me what's happened."

"All right. All right," said Starkey. "I figure since those bastards attacked us here the other night that Berry's declared open war with us. Right?"

"It looks that way to me," Slocum agreed.

"So I thought that we ought to have it stated right out in the open between us real clear and direct, you know? I rode over to Berry's place. I meant to just tell him that. Just that. I was going to say something like, you started the war, so anything goes from here on out. I just wanted a clear understanding between me and Berry. That's all."

"So you rode onto Berry's ranch all by yourself," said Slocum.

"Hell," said Starkey. "I just went to talk. That's all."

"You don't look like you just talked."

"Berry wouldn't even come out of the house," Starkey said. "Two cowhands flanked me up to the house, and Jo Jo was waiting on the porch. Jo Jo wouldn't tell Berry that I was there. Instead, all three of them jumped on me."

"You said Berry wouldn't talk to you," Slocum said. "How do you know he even knew you were there?"

"Hell, he knows everything that goes on around that place," said Starkey, "the son of a bitch. Brandy came out of the house while I was taking a pounding. If she heard it from inside, he must have. He—aw, hell, I guess I don't know for sure."

Slocum sighed and scratched his head. "You want a cup of coffee?" he asked. "I got some fresh."

"Yeah," said Starkey. "Thanks."

Slocum poured two cups and carried one over to Starkey. "You're probably right about Berry though," he said. "So what did she do?"

"Brandy?"

"Well, who else 'she'?"

"Brandy tried to stop them from pounding on me," said Starkey. He sipped the hot coffee. "She did get Jo Jo distracted enough that I managed to get a good swift kick to his balls. That kind of ended the fight.''

Slocum chuckled. ''If that's how the fight ended,'' he said, ''then I'd say you won.''

Starkey laughed a little then too. ''You know,'' he said, ''I hadn't thought about it, but I reckon you're right about that.''

'' 'Course, you don't look like you won,'' Slocum mumbled.

Just then Slocum heard the sound of approaching hooves, and he stepped back over into the doorway for a look down the lane. ''Rider coming,'' he said. He waited a little, then added, ''It's Miss Berry.''

''Brandy?'' said Starkey.

''Yup.''

''Alone?''

''Looks like it.''

Slocum stepped out onto the porch to meet the visitor just as she pulled up and dismounted. She gave Slocum a look.

''You,'' she said.

''Yeah,'' said Slocum. ''Me.''

''Is Sammy here?'' she asked.

Slocum gestured over his shoulder. ''Inside,'' he said.

''Is he all right?''

''He's been better,'' said Slocum, ''but I reckon he'll mend. After all, he won the fight, didn't he?''

Brandy rushed past Slocum and on into the house. Slocum leaned back against the wall to wait and listen. Just inside the door, Brandy hesitated and looked across the room at Starkey. ''Sammy?'' she said.

''What are you doing here?'' Starkey asked.

"I was worried about you," she said. "I came to see how you're doing."

"Aw, I'm all right," Starkey said. "Hell, me and Slocum figured out that I won the damn fight. 'Course, I had a little help from you. Did I thank you for that?"

"I don't remember," she said.

"Well, thanks," said Starkey.

"Sammy," she said, "just what the hell did you think you were doing anyhow?"

"I just wanted to talk to your old man." he said. "That's all."

"What about?"

"About the war between us," said Starkey. "That's what."

"What war?"

"Brandy, don't try to tell me that you don't know what's going on here," Starkey said. "Your old man sent some boys over here the other night to try to burn me out. He's declared war, and I ain't going to run. It's going to be a fight to the finish."

"I don't believe that Daddy did that," Brandy said.

"Who else?"

"Maybe Jo Jo brought some of the boys over here," she said, "but if he did, he did it on his own. I know Daddy wants to buy your ranch, but he wouldn't resort to that kind of thing. I know he wouldn't."

"Well," said Starkey, "you believe what you want. I'll do what I have to do."

Brandy walked over to the table where the bowl of water sat and dipped a towel into the water. She wrung it out and moved back toward Starkey.

"Sit down," she said. "Let me wash your face. You look terrible."

Starkey sat. "Just think what I'd look like if I'd lost," he said. Brandy wiped his forehead. "Ouch."

"Oh, hush," she said. "If you can take all that fighting, you can take this."

"Brandy," said Starkey, "you hadn't ought to even be here."

"Why not?"

"I'm at war with your father. What would he say if he knew you were here?"

"I don't know," she said, "and I don't care. When I get back home, I'm going to have a talk with him about this so-called war and about that no-good Jo Jo. Right now, just be still."

"I don't want to be still," said Starkey, standing up. He put his hands on Brandy's shoulders and pulled her close.

"Sammy," she protested, but she didn't pull back, didn't struggle.

He pressed his lips hard against hers and slid his arms around her to pull her even closer. He thrilled as he felt her lovely breasts press against his chest. He let his hands slide down her back, and he rubbed the graceful curve just above the waistband of her jeans. She moaned out loud and thrust her hips forward, grinding into his crotch. Starkey felt his cock rise to the occasion. "Ohh," he said.

Out on the porch, Slocum heard the unmistakable sounds. He tugged his hat down by the front edge of the brim and ambled off the porch and toward the corral. He was definitely not needed at the house. He wondered what would become of this. Starkey was about to engage in a real shooting war with Ben Berry, and here he was about to roll in the sack with Brandy Berry, old Ben's daughter. It didn't seem quite right on the one hand. On the other hand, he sure didn't blame Starkey for what he was about to do—to Ben or to Brandy.

Back inside, Brandy and Starkey had both undressed, and Starkey was lying flat on his back in bed. Brandy had crawled between his legs from the foot of the bed. One hand fondled his balls while the other gripped his rock-hard cock. She squeezed as it bucked and throbbed in her grip.

"I think it wants to get away," she said.

"Oh, no," said Starkey. "Not unless you've got another place to put it."

"What kind of place?" she asked.

"Oh, someplace dark and smooth and damp. Some warm, comfortable place."

Brandy stroked the cock up and down, and Starkey started to hump her hand in spite of himself.

"Don't get in a hurry," she said, and she shot out her tongue and flicked the head of his cock. He shuddered all over and moaned out loud.

Brandy started slithering her way upward, kissing and licking his belly and chest as she moved. Her face over his, she pressed open lips down against his eagerly awaiting mouth and probed with her tongue. At the same time, she held his cock tight, and she rubbed its head in between the wet lips of her cunt. Starkey thrust upward, but she still held the cock. She rubbed the head up and down the length of her wet slit.

Then all of a sudden she placed it just right, just at the entrance to the pleasure passage, and she pressed herself downward, taking the full length of the cock into her warm, wet depths.

"Ahh," Starkey groaned with pleasure. He thrust upward, trying to shove himself in even deeper. Then he withdrew in order to drive in again. He humped hard and fast, slapping his pelvis against hers again and again. At last he slowed and stopped.

Brandy drew her knees up under her, then sat up straight. She slid her ass along his body, riding the rod forward, then back. Back and forth she rode, faster and faster until she stopped suddenly with a shout of intense pleasure. She threw back her head and shook her hair. Then she looked down at him and let herself fall forward.

She kissed him, a deep, wet kiss. "That was wonderful," she said. "I think I'll do it again."

"Be my guest," said Starkey. "Do it again."

She did. Five times more. After the sixth time, she lay heavily on his chest, breathing deeply. His hands roamed over her back and down to her bare ass. He squeezed a round cheek in each hand.

"I think it's my turn now," he said. "Don't you?"

"Anything you say, Sammy."

He gripped her hard, then rolled them over until he was on top. He moved slowly at first, a slow, controlled, gentle, and rhythmic fuck. She smiled, closed her eyes, and responded with her own thrusts. He built up slowly, moving ever faster and faster until he was driving desperately into her, pounding, slapping again and again.

She was no longer smiling. Her eyes were opened wide and so was her mouth. She was meeting his thrusts with her own and calling out at each slap of their bodies.

"Oh. Oh. Oh."

"Ah," said Starkey. "I'm going to come."

"Yes," she said. "Yes. Do it. Do it."

He drove into her a few more times, and then he felt the sudden release from deep inside him. He drove into her as far as he could and let it gush. He spurted again and again until the thick cream filled her and ran out, coating her upper thighs. At last he relaxed heavily on top of her, pressing her into the bed, and they both laughed in their joy.

Outside at the corral, Slocum lit a cigar. He drew the smoke in deeply, then let out a blue-gray cloud that rose above his head and slowly dissipated in the slight breeze. He wondered what Ben Berry and Jo Jo were up to. He hoped that his boss had enjoyed a good fuck, and he thought about Veronica, wondering what would be a good time to pay her another visit.

9

"Word's out that there's going to be an all-out war between you and Berry," Chilly said to Starkey. "Dammit, boy, I know you're in the right, but you know as well as I do that you can't stand up to Ben Berry and his whole damn crew. Not just you and Slocum. Not just the two of you."

"Chilly," said Starkey, "I ain't running out. Is that what you want me to do? Run? Well, I ain't going to do it. I can't do it. I ain't made that way."

Kirkpatrick turned in exasperation toward Slocum, who was lounging against the counter in the general store.

"You tell him," he said. "He feels like he's got a stake here— a home or something, and besides that, he's crazy. But you got no stake, and I got no reason yet to suspect you of being crazy. Tell him to take Berry's money and get the hell out of here.''

''You know that much about him,'' said Slocum, ''you know he won't listen to me.''

''Hell, you or no one else,'' Kirkpatrick grumbled. ''Well, Sam, you didn't ride in here to listen to my advice. What did you come for?''

''Dynamite,'' said Starkey.

Kirkpatrick's eyes opened wide, and his jaw dropped.

''What the hell do you want with that?'' he asked.

''You sure you want to know?'' Slocum asked.

''No, I ain't,'' said Chilly, ''but tell me anyhow.''

''War's been declared,'' said Starkey. ''Ain't you heard?''

Brandy Berry stormed into the big ranch house on the Berry spread. She stopped just inside the door and looked around the big living room.

''Daddy,'' she called. There was no answer. She stomped across the room to a closed door, hesitated a moment, then jerked it open. Inside the study, Berry looked up from behind his large desk.

''We have to talk,'' Brandy said.

''What's the matter?'' Berry asked.

''Sam Starkey claims that you sent Jo Jo and some of the boys over to his place to try to burn him out,'' she said. ''Is that true?''

''You been talking to Starkey?'' Berry asked.

''I just told you,'' she said. ''Is it true?''

''When did you talk to him?''

''Yesterday afternoon. Now I want to know—''

"Where?" snapped Berry.

"Where? What does it matter where? I talked to him, and he said that Jo Jo and some of the boys rode out to his place after dark and set his house on fire."

"Where did you talk to Starkey?" Berry insisted.

"He rode over here to talk to you," said Brandy, "and Jo Jo and two of the boys jumped on him. I rode over to his place later to find out if he was okay."

Berry stood up quickly. He walked around the desk to step up close to his daughter and stare her hard in the face.

"You rode over to Starkey's house?" he said. "Dammit, Brandy, that was a fool thing to do."

"Why?" she said. "Are you afraid he'll shoot me because of what you've done to him? Daddy, I told him that I didn't believe you did that. I said that if Jo Jo did it, he did it on his own without you knowing anything about it. Oh, Daddy, you let me make a fool of myself defending you."

"All right," said Berry. "All right. Now, listen to me, and listen good. In the first place, I don't need you or anyone defending me. Let's get that straight." Brandy just stared at her father with a deep pout on her face. Berry went on. "Now, about Starkey's place," he said. "It's a small place. Some might say it's not important. But it's the only valley ranch left that I don't own, and I mean to have it."

"No matter what it takes?"

"No matter," said Berry. "Dammit, girl, I made him a fair offer. More than fair. It's not as if I was trying to steal the place."

"But if a man owns something," Brandy said, "no

one has a right to try to make him sell it.''

"Brandy, in this country a man goes after what he wants. If he's strong enough, he gets it.''

"Is that how you got all those other ranches?''

"It's the only way anyone gets anything. I guess I tried to protect you for too long. It's time for you to grow up, kid. Look at the world the way it really is.''

Brandy looked long and hard at her father, and for the first time in her life she felt as if she didn't even know him—had never really known him. Her mind formed a sentence calculated to cut him deep. *I crawled in his bed, and he screwed me,* her mind said, but she couldn't quite get her mouth to say the words out loud. She was afraid that she had already pushed her luck to its limits. She turned and stalked out of the room.

Back at the SS, Slocum hauled back on the reins to halt the wagon. While Starkey hefted the box of explosives out of the wagon, Slocum went to fetch a shovel out of the barn. When he returned, Starkey had already broken open the crate. He had paced over to a spot where the end of the lane came into the yard.

"About here?'' he asked.

"Over to your right,'' said Slocum. "I don't think we want to be riding over it.''

Starkey sidestepped until he was off the lane.

"You're right,'' he said. "I must have been thinking they'd be here tonight and we'd blow it before we ever ride out again.''

"Well, we might,'' said Slocum, "but we can't be sure, now, can we?''

"About here?"

"Looks good to me," said Slocum.

He dug a shallow hole, and Starkey laid in a stick of dynamite. Then Slocum covered it over again. Starkey jabbed a stake into the ground just over the stick. A strip of white rag was tied to the top end of the stake. Before they were done, there were a dozen such stakes placed at strategic spots around the yard in front of the house.

They were spotted around with two things in mind. First the two men recalled as best they could just about where the Berry riders had been when they rode in at night the last two times. Second, the dynamite sticks were placed so that Starkey and Slocum would have good straight shots at them through the windows from inside the house. The last stake placed, Starkey straightened up and wiped his forehead with his sleeve.

"The bastards come around again," he said, "they'll get a hell of a surprise."

"Yeah," said Slocum. "I reckon. Can I make a suggestion, boss?"

"Sure," said Starkey. "Don't I always listen to you?"

"Your record ain't very good so far," said Slocum.

"Never mind that," Starkey snapped. "What's your suggestion?"

"We start sleeping in shifts."

"Hell, Slocum, I was just about to say that myself."

• • •

Slocum was sitting on the porch with his Winchester across his knees, listening to the sounds of the night. Bugs chirred, and in the distance, coyotes yelped. He judged it to be somewhere around midnight. Starkey was in the house, presumably asleep. Slocum pulled a cigar out of his pocket and was reaching for a match, when something made him hesitate. He wasn't at all sure what it was at first. He waited.

Then his ears defined for him the faint sound of horses' hooves in the distance. The sound came from the road. He waited, listening as they came closer. In the darkness he couldn't see the far end of the lane, where it came into the ranch from the road, but he thought he could tell by the sound when the riders turned in and headed toward the house. He stood up and moved to the door. At last he could see faint movement in the distance, and he went on inside. He stepped to the window on the right of the door.

"Starkey," he said. "Wake up."

Starkey sat up straight in bed.

"What is it?" he said.

"Riders coming."

Starkey pulled on his boots, grabbed his rifle, and went to the other window to look out.

"I don't see anything," he said in a harsh whisper.

"Riding in on the lane," said Slocum.

They waited another quiet, tense moment. Then Starkey spoke again.

"I see the bastards," he said. "You want the first shot?"

"You can have it," said Slocum. "Sight in on that

flag nearest the lane. I'll watch the riders and say when.''

Starkey cranked a shell into the chamber of his Winchester, then laid the rifle across the windowsill and took careful aim.

"I got it," he said. "I'm ready."

"Hold it," said Slocum. He watched as the riders came closer. He counted six, and he thought that he could recognize Jo Jo Darby in the lead. Just behind Jo Jo, two others rode side by side, and the other three rode almost abreast in a third row. Slocum allowed Jo Jo to ride past the trap. Then the two behind him were just about beside it.

"Now," he said, and Starkey pulled the trigger. The rifle cracked and was almost instantly followed by a deafening blast and a blinding flash. The air was filled with a giant dust cloud and clods of earth banged and battered against the house. Jo Jo Darby, for indeed it was he in the lead, was knocked forward out of the saddle. From their places at the windows neither Starkey nor Slocum could see any of the other riders. They could hear the shouts and screams and the loud cursing.

Slocum tried to get a bead on Jo Jo, but the cowboy had rolled clear up against the front edge of the porch and was hidden from Slocum's sight. Starkey squinted through the dust cloud until he spotted another flag, and he sighted in and fired again. There was a second explosion and a second cloud of dust. There were more screams and shouts.

"Dammit, boss," said Slocum. "That's enough. I can't tell what the hell's going on out there."

As the noise of the second explosion faded, Slocum thought that he could hear the sound of escaping horses' hooves. He couldn't tell how many. More than one though, he thought. But maybe only two. He couldn't tell. The dust was still heavy in the air outside, and that combined with the darkness of the night made it impossible for him to see anything.

"What do we do now?" Starkey whispered.

"Wait," said Slocum.

They waited. Eventually the dust settled. Slocum made out one horse and one man in the lane. Both were down and still. He could see nothing else. No one moving.

"Keep watching, boss," he said. "I'm going out the back and sneak around the house."

"Okay," said Starkey.

Slocum hurried across the room and out the back door. Keeping close to the house, he moved to a back corner, then along the wall to the front corner. He hesitated a moment, then peeked carefully around the corner. He saw nothing moving. The last he had seen of Jo Jo Darby, the man had been hugging earth just at the front edge of the porch. He could still be there.

Slocum readied his rifle and ran to the front edge of the porch. Jo Jo was not there. He walked out now more boldly to look around the yard. There was no one to be seen except the one downed rider and his horse.

"Starkey," he called out. "They're all gone. All but one, and he ain't going nowhere."

Starkey came out the front door and walked out to

stand beside Slocum. He looked at the two dead men and horse.

"You mean that's all we got with two explosions?" he asked.

"Well," said Slocum, "that's all we killed outright. I imagine there's some others hurt. Jo Jo got blowed off his horse, but him and the horse are both gone now. It's hard to tell what happened back behind the blast. If nothing else, I bet there's some ears ringing."

"We said they'd be surprised," said Starkey.

"They were," said Slocum. "But next time they won't try that approach. We got to really get watchful now."

"Yeah," said Starkey.

"Unless—"

"Unless what?"

"Unless we stop waiting for them to attack us and move in on Berry's house ourselves."

"They sure won't be expecting that," said Starkey.

"They especially won't be expecting it tonight," Slocum said.

"Aw, now, I don't know about that, Slocum," Starkey said. "I need to think about that for a while."

"What's to think about?"

"Well, attacking a man in his own home—I don't know."

"Shit," said Slocum. "You ain't thinking about Berry. You're thinking about his daughter."

10

Back at Berry's ranch, Jo Jo and the others came limping in, and Berry was there on the porch to meet them. It was obvious immediately to Berry that something had gone very wrong. There was a horse without a rider, there was one rider barely keeping himself in the saddle, and there was a horse and rider missing. As Jo Jo rode up close to the porch, Berry stepped forward.

"What the hell happened?" he demanded.

"They was waiting for us," said Jo Jo. "The bastards. And they used dynamite."

"Some of you boys take care of the hurt ones," Berry said. "And put up the horses. Do we need to send for Doc Burns?"

"I don't think so," said Jo Jo. "We can patch these boys up no worse than they're hurt."

"All right, then," said Berry. "Get to it."

All the riders except Jo Jo, who dismounted and stayed at the porch with Berry, rode off toward the corral and bunkhouse. Jo Jo stepped up to the edge of the porch.

"Son of a bitches blew me clean out of the saddle," he said. "I never expected no dynamite. Hell, my ears is still ringing."

"Who's missing?" Berry asked.

"Charley Sims," said Jo Jo. He sat down on the edge of the porch. "They blowed him all to hell. Him and his horse."

"Dammit," Berry snapped. "Just two men."

"They had dynamite," said Jo Jo.

"Everything's changed now," said Berry. "We have to take a whole new approach to this problem. And the problem is that Slocum. Without Slocum, Starkey wouldn't be any more of a problem than any of the others were."

"I can take them, Mr. Berry," said Jo Jo. "Now that I know what they're up to, I can take them. I'll take more of the boys next time. Twenty or so. We'll come at them from all sides, and we won't come in too close from the front. That's where they got us with the dynamite. We go at them right, we can get the bastards."

"Yeah," said Berry. "Yeah, I'm sure. For now, forget about it. Go get some sleep. I'll come up with something."

Just inside the house, Brandy was pressed against the wall beside the door, listening to every word. When she realized that her father had dismissed Jo Jo and would likely be coming back in the house, she stood very still and kept quiet. When the door opened, she was hiding behind it. Berry shut the door behind himself and walked across the room to his study without looking back over his shoulder. He shut himself in the study. He hadn't seen her.

She had tried to argue with Sam Starkey about her father. He wasn't like that, she had said. He wouldn't do those things. Jo Jo Darby must have been acting on his own. Now there was no mistake. She knew the truth. There was no way around it. There was no way she could any longer defend him. He was a crook and a bully and very nearly a murderer. She had spied on him. She had listened to his conversation with Jo Jo. She had heard it all for herself.

She didn't know what to do. She had to admit to herself that for some time now there had been a doubt in her mind, a fear that the things Starkey was saying were true. But now that the doubts and fears had become certainty, she was devastated by the knowledge. She thought about going to Starkey, leaving her father's house for good, but Starkey had not invited her. She went upstairs to her room and locked herself in.

It was just after breakfast at the SS. Starkey had cooked and served the meal, and Slocum was washing the dishes. It was Starkey who first heard the riders approaching. He picked up his Winchester and stood at the window, watching.

"Riders coming, Slocum," he said.

Slocum dried his hands on his jeans and went after his own rifle. He took up his position at the other window. By then the riders were closer.

"That's Berry in the lead," said Starkey.

"They ain't coming to fight," said Slocum. "Berry wants to talk."

"How can you tell?"

"It just makes sense," said Slocum. "That's all."

"I'll go out," said Starkey. He put his rifle against the wall and walked to the door. "You stay where you are," he added. "Just in case."

"Exactly what I'd have said." Slocum kept his rifle laid across the windowsill. As Berry, with two riders flanking him, rode up to the porch and halted his mount, Starkey stepped out the door. Berry held up his hands. He glanced toward the window where Slocum had him covered.

"I came to talk, Starkey," he said. Nodding toward the window, he added, "You don't need that."

"We'll just stay like we are," said Starkey. "Say what you came to say and ride out of here."

"Can I step down?"

"You ain't going to be here that long," Starkey said.

"I understand that you came over to my place the other day for a talk," Berry said. "I didn't get to see you that time, so I came over here to you. Can't we have a friendly talk?"

"You know what happened to me that time too," Starkey said. "Why shouldn't I do the same thing to you?"

"That was Jo Jo," said Berry. "If I'd have been there, it wouldn't have happened."

"Yeah. Sure. Say your piece and get out of here."

"I don't want to fight you, Starkey," Berry said. "Hell, my daughter's been over here to see you. I think she's sweet on you. No telling what went on over here behind my back. Why don't you sell me your place—for a good price—and come courting right out in the open. You and Brandy get married, you'll wind up owning everything one of these days anyhow."

"Well, I'll be damned," said Starkey. "Hey, Slocum. Did you hear that? This sorry bastard is worse than I thought. Hell, he's trying to bargain with his own daughter."

"I heard," said Slocum. "You want me to shoot him?"

"No, I guess not," said Starkey. "Not just yet. Berry, I don't want to inherit your ranch. I don't want to own the whole damn valley. And I sure as hell don't want you for a father-in-law. I'm going to tell you this one more time. My ranch is not for sale. Not to you and not for any price.

"The way I see it, you got two choices. You can go on back home and forget the whole thing, and I will too. No more fighting. You own the whole valley except for my little place. Let it go at that."

"I don't like it," said Berry. "What's my other choice?"

"War," said Starkey.

"Come on," said Berry. "Hell, there's only two of you. You can't fight a war with just the two of you."

"We been standing up all right so far," said Starkey.

"I've just been playing with you," said Berry. "You don't know how rough it can get."

"You don't either," said Slocum from inside the house. "Let me shoot the son of a bitch for you right now, boss. Then the war would be over."

"He might not ask me the next time, Berry," said Starkey. "He might just go ahead and shoot. I think you'd better get on out of here while you still can."

Berry jerked his reins to turn his horse.

"Let's go, boys," he said. He and his two cowboys turned their mounts and started to ride toward the road. Berry slowed and looked back over his shoulder. "I understand you got some cows coming, Starkey," he said. "It'll be too bad for you if they don't show up." He and the other two spurred their horses and headed out at a fair clip. Slocum's trigger finger had an itch that he finally decided had to be scratched. He fired a round over the heads of the retreating riders, and they doubled their speed instantly.

Starkey stood on the porch a moment longer, watching them race away. Then he turned and walked back inside. Slocum had already put down his rifle and gone back to the dishes.

"Well, boss?" he said.

"You were right again," said Starkey. "We'll go tonight."

"Now you're talking," Slocum said.

11

A young bull calf, feeling sprightly, took off from the small herd of cattle, and the hefty foreman of the crew shouted out an order.

"Go get him, Panhandle," he called.

A young cowboy riding a small pinto unleashed his lariat and raced after the calf. The horse knew his business as well as did his rider, and they turned the calf back into the herd in quick time. Panhandle slowed his pinto and rode up alongside the foreman.

"How was that, Dusty?" he asked.

"Oh," said Dusty, "I reckon it'll do."

"It'll do?" said Panhandle. "You never seen better. I told you I got the best little cow pony in the business, and just now I showed you. Admit it."

"She's a good little pony," Dusty admitted, but nothing more.

"Hell," said Panhandle, "you're just being stubborn. You just don't want to admit that I'm right. You never seen a pony as good as this one."

"Well, let's find out how well she travels, then," Dusty said.

"What do you mean?"

"You know your way to Dead Dog?"

"I've been there," Panhandle said. "It's been a few years, but I reckon I can find the place."

"Well, ride on ahead, then, and see if you can look up Sam Starkey on the SS Ranch. Tell him I figure us to be three—four days out. Likely he'll want to ride back out with you to meet the herd."

"You want me to take off right now?"

"Yeah, but be careful," Dusty said. "I got the feeling that Starkey's expecting some trouble. That's why he wants to meet us out here and ride on in with the herd."

"Don't worry, boss," said Panhandle. "I'll watch my ass, and I'll be back here with ol' Starkey in just about two shakes."

Brandy was shut up in her bedroom. She wasn't crying. She had told herself that she wouldn't do that. She wouldn't let it happen. But she was upset. She was being forced to accept the fact that her father was the worst of the things that had been said about him, the things that, yes, she herself had imagined about him and then forced out of her mind.

She felt she could no longer stay with him. She could no longer live with a man who would steal, a man who would bully other men off their own property, a man who in his own words would stop at nothing to get what he wanted. Would he even murder, she wondered, and she could not bring herself to answer the question, for she was afraid of what the answer would be.

But where could she go? She had no way of providing for herself. She had lived all her life with her father. She had lived all her life off her father. She didn't know how to make a living for herself. It had never before occurred to her that she would ever have to earn her own way. An image of the girls in town who worked for Madame Veronica at the Dead Dog Saloon came into her mind, and it horrified her.

Then there was Sammy. She could live with Sammy. She knew she could. She could love him easily. Perhaps she did love him. She told herself that she couldn't have done what she had done with Sammy if she did not love him. She wasn't that kind.

But Sammy had never asked her to marry him. He had not even asked her to live with him in sin. She would do that if he asked her. She told herself that she didn't believe in sin anyhow. She would live with Sammy. But he hadn't asked her. Not even after she had flung herself at him and on him and all over him. He hadn't asked.

She wondered if she could go to Sammy and ask him if he would have her. She would have to swallow her pride to do that. And then, what if Sammy didn't want her? Would he tell her so to her face? And then what would she do? She felt tears welling up inside her head, tears of anger and frustration and humiliation, and she fought hard to hold them back.

Panhandle rode into Dead Dog dead tired. He found the sight of the Dead Dog Saloon to be irresistible, and so he tied his pinto pony to the rail out front and went inside. Stepping up to the bar, he ordered himself a beer. He knew he didn't have much time, but a quick beer wouldn't hurt anything. Besides, he and the pony both needed at least a short rest before going on to search for the SS Ranch.

He took a long swallow of the beer before he set the glass back down on the bar. Dusty had said that he thought that Starkey was expecting trouble, so Panhandle figured he ought to be careful what he said and to whom he said it. But he didn't know where the SS Ranch was, so he would have to find out from someone. He thought about asking the big bartender. Bartenders, he told himself, are usually pretty good about keeping things to themselves.

He was about to open his mouth and ask the question, when a cowboy came through the batwing doors and walked up to lean his elbows on the bar not four feet from where Panhandle stood.

"Whiskey," he said.

Waiting for his order to be filled, he glanced at Panhandle. A look of recognition spread across his face. "Hey," he said. "Hey there, old buddy."

Panhandle looked up at the cowboy's face for the first time. "Well, I be damned," he said. "Stinky. It's been a few years, ain't it?"

Stinky picked up the glass that was there in front of him by this time and took a sip. "Yeah," he said. "A few years. You back in these parts to stay?"

"No," said Panhandle. "I'm just passing through. Actually I'm helping to deliver some cows to an old boy. Can you tell me how to find the SS?"

When Panhandle rode out of Dead Dog, headed for the SS according to instructions Stinky had given him, Stinky watched him go. As soon as Panhandle was out of sight, Stinky mounted up and headed for Berry's place. It was a fairly short ride, and soon he was talking to Berry and Jo Jo on the big porch of the Berry house.

"So," Berry was saying, "your old friend was riding to the SS to inform Starkey that his herd is on the way in?"

"Yeah," said Stinky. "That's what it seemed like."

"He was alone?"

"Yup."

"That means that the herd and the other drovers are back on the trail yet," Berry mused. "Did he say how far out they are?"

"No, sir," Stinky said. "Just asked for the way to the SS and said that he was delivering cows. That's all he said."

"You should have found out more," Jo Jo snapped.

"Never mind that, Jo Jo," said Berry. "Listen, Stinky. Here's what I want you to do. Get a fresh horse. Catch up with that cowboy and follow him until you spot that herd. Then get back here lickety-split and let me know where they are, which way they're coming in, and how far out they are. You got that?''

''Yes, sir,'' said Stinky. ''Only—''

''What?'' asked Berry.

''I'm just a cowhand, Mr. Berry. I ain't no gun-fighter. I—''

''I know that, Stinky,'' Berry said. ''I don't want you to do a damn thing except what I said. I don't want you to fight anyone. Okay?''

''Yes, sir,'' said Stinky.

''Go on, now.''

Slocum was sitting on the porch, smoking a cigar and generally enjoying a fine day. Starkey was somewhere inside, doing something. Slocum didn't really care. He was just taking it easy. He and Starkey had already planned a quick raid on Berry's place for late that night. There was no need to think about it further or worry about it. It was a good time to rest and relax.

Then he saw a rider at the far end of the lane, turning in from the road. A man alone. He waited a moment, then got up and stepped to the door. Still watching the approaching rider, he spoke to Starkey over his shoulder.

''Rider coming,'' he said.

Starkey stepped over to the door and squinted his eyes, looking past Slocum. He reached over for his rifle and held it casually down at his side. Slocum was wearing his Colt revolver. Both men stepped out onto the porch to wait.

''Recognize him?'' Slocum asked. The rider was

close enough by this time for them to see him fairly well.

"I don't think I've ever seen him before," said Starkey. "He looks friendly enough."

The rider on the pinto stopped a polite distance away and touched the brim of his hat.

"This the SS?" he asked.

"It is," said Starkey.

"They call me Panhandle. I'm riding for Mr. Howard. I'm looking for Mr. Starkey."

"I'm Sam Starkey. This here is Slocum. Climb down, Panhandle. Come on in the house."

"I'll take care of your pony," said Slocum.

Starkey led Panhandle into the house as Slocum took the pinto to the corral. Inside, Starkey gave Panhandle a seat at the table, then poured two cups of coffee. He put them on the table and sat across from the cowboy.

"What's the story?" he asked.

Panhandle sipped his coffee.

"Mighty good," he said. "Thanks. Well, sir, Dusty, he's the ramrod for this trip, he sent me ahead to tell you that we're just about three—four days out. Told me to hurry in and hurry back out. Said you might want to ride along back with me."

"How's the herd?" Starkey asked just as Slocum stepped through the doorway.

"In good shape," said Panhandle. "We rode easy, and they've fattened up real good."

Slocum poured himself a cup of coffee and sat down with the other two men.

"You lose any?" Starkey asked.

"Nary a one," said Panhandle. "Tell you the truth, Mr. Starkey, it's one of the best drives I've ever been on. It was easy going all the way."

"I'm glad to hear that," Starkey said.

Slocum sipped hot coffee and looked at Starkey over the rim of his cup. It might not be so easy the last leg, he thought. If Berry gets wind of the herd coming into the SS, there could be big trouble. He thought he'd keep his mouth shut though, but then Panhandle spoke up again and showed that he already had some idea of what was what in the valley outside of Dead Dog.

"Dusty said you might be expecting trouble," he said. "Anything to it?"

Starkey and Slocum eyeballed each other.

"You'd best tell him," Slocum said.

"Yeah," said Starkey. "We are having trouble. One of my neighbors has been trying to buy me out. Since I won't sell, he's trying to run me out. It's possible that if he gets wind of this herd coming in, he might try something."

Panhandle shoved his hat back and scratched his head. "I figured it might be something like that," he said. "Mind telling me that neighbor's name?"

"It's Ben Berry," said Starkey.

"Damn," Panhandle said. "I reckon I've done let the cat out of the bag."

"What do you mean?" Slocum asked.

"I seen an old pal of mine on the way through town," Panhandle drawled. "Cowhand named Stinky. I told him what I was doing and asked for directions out here. Some years back, me and Stinky both rode for Berry. I reckon he still does.''

"Is this Stinky a gun hand?'' Slocum asked.

"Hell no,'' Panhandle said. "He's just a cow-poke.''

"He might not have said anything about it, then,'' Slocum opined, "but then again, he might have. I think we'd best act as if Berry knows all about it by now.''

"Yeah,'' said Starkey. "You're right.'' He turned toward Panhandle. "You and the rest of your crew don't need to get caught up in this fight,'' he said. "Me and Slocum can bring the cows on in.''

"Hell, Mr. Starkey,'' Panhandle said, "if I know Dusty, he'll insist on riding all the way in here with them. Dusty never was one to run from a fight, and when he contracts to deliver a herd, he delivers it.''

"All right, then,'' said Starkey. "You know that old mesa east of town?''

"Sure,'' said Panhandle. "Right now it's about halfway between here and where we're at with the herd.''

"If you get there with the herd before we meet up with you,'' Starkey said, "hold up there and wait for us. There's good grass and water there.''

"So you ain't riding back with me?''

"No, but we'll meet you at the mesa.'' Starkey looked at Slocum. "Sound all right to you?''

"Sounds just fine,'' Slocum agreed. He lifted his coffee cup and drained it.

12

It was a bold scheme for just the two of them to attack the Berry place, but they figured that Berry would be overconfident. He would never expect them to attack him. He had them so outnumbered that he would figure all their actions would be defensive. They were right. When they arrived at the Berry spread under cover of deep darkness, they found no sentries posted and no lights burning.

They rode in quietly, watching all around for any signs of anyone who might be up and about. They rode straight to the corral in front of the barn and quietly opened the gate. Then Slocum rode around to the back side of the barn while Starkey headed for the bunkhouse. Back behind the barn, Slocum lit a small fire up close against the wall. Starkey would be doing the same thing to the bunkhouse. It would take a little while for the fires to grow enough for anyone to notice them.

Riding back around the barn, Slocum met Starkey. They nodded at each other, indicating that each had done his job. Together then, they rode toward the front porch of the big ranch house. Slocum struck a match and lit a cigar as Starkey reached into his saddlebags to pull out two sticks of dynamite.

Slocum took a few quick puffs to get the cigar going well. Starkey held one of the sticks out toward him and Slocum took it. He touched the end of the cigar to the fuse. He held it a moment, watching it spark and fizz. Then with a casual underhand toss he pitched it up onto the porch.

Starkey held the second stick out toward Slocum, and Slocum touched the fuse with his cigar end. Just then Homer Drink stepped out the door of the bunkhouse, reaching for his fly. He looked up and saw the two riders over by the big house. He saw the sparks flying from the stick in the one rider's hand. He forgot all about his need to piss and shouted.

"Hey. Who are you?"

He turned and ran back to the bunkhouse door, jerking it open and poking his head in.

"Hey," he called out. "Wake up. There's someone out here."

"We're spotted," said Slocum.

Starkey turned and flung the second dynamite stick toward the bunkhouse. He hadn't planned that. It was a reaction to the shouting of Homer Drink. The cowhands were crowding through the door, but when they

saw the stick with the sparkling fuse, they tried to turn
and crowd their way back inside. The stick fell short.
Then it exploded. A second later the one on the porch
blew.

The silence of the night air was shattered by the
double blast, and the blackness was lit up eerily by
the blinding flashes. Slocum and Starkey turned their
horses almost together and headed for the road. Most
of the Berry ranch horses had stayed in the corral,
even after the gate had been opened, but the explosions frightened them.

They screamed and ran, ran into one another and
into the corral walls. Eventually they all found their
way out of the corral, either through the open gate or
over the walls they had knocked down. Back at the
bunkhouse the cowboys were falling over one another
to get back inside. One of them then noticed the
flames working their way through the cracks in the
back wall.

"Shit," he yelled. "The house is on fire."

Again they ran, stumbling over one another, this
time trying to get out. Most of them were in only their
longjohns. One or two had pulled on boots, and a couple of them had picked up a six-gun.

At the house Ben Berry and Brandy had gone out
the back door and come around to see what they could
see. The porch was a wreck of splinters, and the front
wall of the house was burning in a few places. Berry,
with little success, was shouting for the hands to get
buckets and save the house. Jo Jo, in long underwear
like the rest of the crew, ran up to Berry's side.

"It was Starkey," he said. "Starkey and that damn Slocum."

"Never mind that right now," Berry yelled. "Get those bastards organized and put out the fire on my house."

"What about the bunkhouse?" Jo Jo asked.

"Do as I say, goddammit," Berry shouted. "Do it."

Jo Jo started back toward the hands at the bunkhouse.

"Hey," he called out. "Come on. Get your ass over here with buckets. Hurry it up." He looked back over his shoulder toward Berry. "It was that fucking Starkey," he said. "He used dynamite on us at his place."

Brandy came up beside her father just then. When she had seen that the fire on the front porch wasn't yet big and dangerous, she had gone back inside and gotten dressed. With Berry in a robe and the crew in their long handles, she was the only one on the ranch fully dressed.

"Are you satisfied?" she said.

"What?"

"This is what you wanted, isn't it? A range war with Sam Starkey? Well, it sure as hell looks like you got it, and I hope you're satisfied."

"Brandy," said Berry, "if you're not going to get a bucket and help fight this fire, then get the hell out of the way."

"I will," she said. "I'll get out. I'll get clear out of your way."

• • •

It was daylight before things were more or less under control at Berry's place. The bunkhouse was a total loss, as was the front porch of the main house. The front wall of the main house was damaged, but at least it was still standing. Only a few horses were anywhere in sight, the rest having run off some distance before they settled down. It would take some time to round them up again. The cowhand, exhausted from loss of sleep and fighting the fires, lay around on the ground. Everyone, including Jo Jo and Berry himself, was covered with black soot. Berry called out to Jo Jo, and Jo Jo came hobbling over to him.

"Get ready for a major assault on the SS," Berry said. "Tonight. I aim to get that son of a bitch for doing this to me."

"Uh, boss," said Jo Jo.

"What?" Berry snapped.

"We got two pair of boots, two six-guns, and one Remington rifle among us. Everything else was burned up inside the bunkhouse. We ain't even got no clothes to put on."

"God damn," said Berry. "How did you let this happen? How could just two men do this to us?"

"I bet they got some help from somewhere," said Jo Jo. "I bet there was more than just the two of them."

"Oh, shut up," said Berry. "Go on back— Wait a minute. Look there."

Jo Jo looked toward the road to see Stinky riding toward them.

"At least we got one cowboy with a complete outfit,'' said Berry. They stood silent then until Stinky pulled up and dismounted.

''I'll be jiggered,'' he said. ''What's happened here?''

''Never mind that,'' said Berry. ''What'd you find out?''

''Well,'' said Stinky, looking around, still taking in the evidence of recent disaster, ''I follered ol' Panhandle out to the SS. He went in the house and stayed for a spell. When he left finally, I follered him out to a small herd of cows. There was five other hands out there with the herd.''

''When did he head back for the herd?'' asked Berry.

''It was just after suppertime, I'd say.''

''Alone?'' asked Jo Jo.

''Yeah.''

''So Starkey and Slocum were both still around,'' Berry mused.

''You see anyone else at the SS?'' Jo Jo wanted to know.

''Nary a soul.''

Berry shot a hard sideways glance at Jo Jo, who tried to ignore it.

''Stinky,'' said Berry, ''come inside with me. I'm going to give you a list of stuff we need from Kirkpatrick's in town. Tell him to have it delivered out here just as soon as he can. Then stop by the sheriff's office and tell Dancer to get out here and see me right away. Come on now. I'll make out that list.''

''What're you sending after, boss?'' Jo Jo called to Berry's back as Berry led Stinky toward the house.

Berry glanced back over his shoulder.

"Clothes and guns, you dumb shit," he said.

It was late afternoon by the time Dancer made his way out to the SS. He found Starkey and Slocum both waiting for him on the porch with six-guns strapped on and Winchesters in their hands.

"What the hell are you doing here, Dancer?" Starkey demanded.

"I got a complaint against you from Mr. Berry," the sheriff said. With a groan he started to swing down out of the saddle.

"Just keep your seat," said Starkey. "You won't be staying long."

Dancer settled back into the saddle. "Now, looky here," he said. "You can't go around blowing up the homes of decent respectable folks and not expect to have to answer to the law."

"Someone's home get blowed up?" Slocum asked.

"You know damn well," said Dancer.

"Suppose you tell us just what we're being accused of," Starkey said.

"We got a right to hear that," said Slocum, "ain't we?"

"Last night you two rode over to Berry's place and dynamited the house and set fire to the barn and the bunkhouse. Turned the horses out too. That's what, as if you didn't know."

"That sounds bad," said Slocum. "Was anyone hurt?"

"No," said Dancer. "Luckily. But the house was heavily damaged and the barn and bunkhouse was both completely destroyed. Destruction of property is a serious offense.''

''I got a question for you, Sheriff,'' said Starkey. ''You know, my place has been attacked a couple of times, and I went to you to complain. I told you that Berry was behind it, and you didn't do a damned thing. How come when he gets attacked and blames me, you come out here ready to arrest me?''

''Did someone claim to actully see us?'' Slocum asked.

''It's known that you have got it in for Berry,'' said Dancer, ''and it's known that you recently bought some dynamite.''

''It's also known that Berry wants my place,'' said Starkey.

''It looks more and more to me,'' said Slocum, ''like you're in Berry's back pocket. How's it smell back there?''

''Damn you, Slocum,'' said Dancer. His hand moved toward the butt of the revolver on his hip.

''Try it, Dancer,'' said Slocum.

Dancer slowly moved his hand back to the horn of his saddle and let it rest there.

''You're both under arrest,'' he said. ''Are you going to come along with me peaceable like, or am I going to have to come back with a posse?''

''I got a question for you now, Dancer,'' said Slocum.

Dancer was so nervous by this time that the sweat was rolling down the sides of his round face.

''What?'' he said. ''What question?''

"How fast can that horse of yours run with your fat ass on his back?"

"What?"

"You think he can outrun a slug from a Winchester rifle?"

Dancer jerked the reins to turn his mount and kicked it hard in the sides. He headed for the road as fast as the poor beast could carry his fat ass.

13

Brandy packed a few changes of clothes in a blanket roll. She could always come back for the rest of her things, she told herself, but right at the moment she just wanted to get the hell out and fast. She probably didn't need all those other things anyhow. It had all been bought with her father's money, money that by this time was seeming more and more dirty to her.

She tied up the roll and threw it over her shoulder, going out of her room, down the stairs, and out the back door of the house. She hated to have to depend on her father for anything anymore, but she needed a horse and saddle, and she told herself that she was entitled to at least that. It would be the last thing she would take from him anyhow.

She had just rounded the front corner of the house

and was headed for the corral. The fences were up again and most of the horses were back. There were even a few undamaged saddles there on the fence. She would help herself to what she needed and get the hell out of Ben Berry's life forever.

Her face felt hot and flushed with anger and resentment. She didn't know where she was going except away. She was looking at the ground, not where she was going, and suddenly she realized that she was about to run into someone. She looked up to see Jo Jo blocking her path.

"Well now, little missy," Jo Jo said through a leering grin, "where you headed for?"

"It's none of your damn business," she said. "Get the hell out of my way."

She tried to walk around him, but he stepped in front of her again.

"That ain't no way for a lady to talk," he said, "especially when a man's come courting."

Brandy wrinkled her face in disgust.

"Don't make me puke," she said.

Jo Jo grabbed her by the shoulders and pulled her toward him. She struggled, but he was too strong for her. He pulled her close, then wrapped his arms around her and held her tight. She tried to get a leg in between his legs so she could raise it up and smash his balls, but he was holding her too close. She turned her face away from his, but she could feel his hot, moist breath and smell its rankness.

"Let me go, you bastard," she said.

"I'm going to get me a little kiss," he said, "and that's just for starters."

"Let go. Damn you."

Just then Jo Jo felt a hard slap to his head that knocked his hat off, and almost immediately someone had a fistful of his hair and was jerking him backward. He staggered, lost his balance, and fell hard on his back. Looking up wide-eyed, he saw the massive form of Ben Berry looming over him.

"Get up," roared Berry.

Jo Jo scooted backward on his ass.

"Mr. Berry," he said. "It ain't what you think. Hell, she was trying to run away. I just stopped her for you. That's all."

"Get on your feet," said Berry.

Jo Jo stood cautiously, and no sooner was he up than Berry slapped him hard with the back of his hand. Jo Jo staggered sideways, and Berry followed, slapping again and again. At last Jo Jo fell again.

"Now, get the hell out of here," said Berry. "You're fired. If I ever see you again, I'll kill you."

Jo Jo's right hand reached for his sidearm, but Berry stepped on it, pressing it against both the revolver's handle and the ground. Jo Jo screamed in agony. Finally Berry eased up. Jo Jo jerked his hand out of the way and held it with his left. Berry kicked the revolver away.

"Get up and get out," he said.

Whimpering audibly, Jo Jo got to his feet once more and cowered away toward the corral. Berry leaned over to pick up the handgun and then held it at his side as he watched Jo Jo saddle a horse, mount up, and ride away. He thought about the scene that had just taken place, and he thought about what his daughter had just gone through. Then he considered what she might have been forced to endure had he not come along when he did.

He wondered what he had become. He was suddenly ashamed of himself and of the years he had lost when he should have been paying more attention to his daughter and thinking more about her future. He wondered what sort of future she would have now. What if something were to happen to him and she were left alone to deal with the likes of Jo Jo?

"Brandy," he said, "I'm sorry. I should have run him off long ago. I should have—"

"You should never have hired him in the first place," she said.

Berry looked at the ground. He couldn't bring himself to look his daughter in the face.

"You're right," he said. "Of course. I—I don't know what's become of me."

Brandy saw a glimmer of hope for the first time since all the trouble had begun. She stepped up in front of her father and tried to look him in the face, but he was still looking down at the ground. She put a hand on his shoulder.

"Daddy?" she said. "Daddy, I'm glad you came along when you did."

She smiled, but at the same time a tear rolled down her cheek. She put her arms around him and hugged him close.

"Daddy," she said, "it's not too late. Call off the war. Leave Sammy alone. You don't have to own the whole valley."

Berry held her for a moment, remaining silent, in

deep thought. He was dealing with feelings he had repressed for a long time. It wasn't easy to let them out again.

"It's too late," he said. "I've already sent some boys out to intercept his herd."

"Oh, Daddy. Daddy, you can stop them."

For the first time, he looked her in the face, and he saw the tears, and he remembered her from years ago when she had been his little girl sitting on his knee.

"Yeah," he said. "You're right. I can stop them."

"I'll go with you," she said.

"No, darling," he said. "There could be trouble if I don't get there fast enough. I don't want you to get hurt. You stay here. And don't worry. I'll take care of it. I promise you."

She watched as he saddled a horse and rode out, and for the first time in a long time she was proud of him. She had always loved him, but now, once again, she was proud. He would stop the war, and everything would be all right again.

Jo Jo rode off the Berry ranch in a rage. He was afraid of Berry, a big and powerful man in every sense. Berry could pound him to mush, and he could out-shoot him. He could also buy up the law and as many gun hands as he wanted. He was not a man to mess with, but then, Jo Jo told himself, neither was Jo Jo Darby. What Jo Jo lacked in power and influence, he could make up for in sneakiness. He was not above laying an ambush and shooting a man in the back.

He hated Berry. He had been humiliated by the old man in front of that stuck-up bitch Brandy. He had thought that he could marry Brandy and eventually, when old Ben died, Brandy would inherit the valley. As her husband, he would own it. He would be the big man. Now that possibility was gone.

Well, he thought, maybe he would never own the valley, but he would kill Berry for what he had done, and he would find an opportunity to take his pleasure on Brandy. He would at least do those two things before he left the valley behind him.

His immediate problem was getting a gun. Berry had disarmed him back at the ranch just before running him off, and everything else he owned had been lost in the fire. Lucky that Berry had ordered out that load of supplies. At least he had clothes on his back. But how to get a gun?

Then he realized that the gunnies that Berry had sent out after Starkey's herd would not know what had happened back at the ranch. As far as they were concerned, he was still their foreman. He would ride out after them, get a gun from one of them, and then get on with his business. He topped a rise, slowed a bit, and looked back over his shoulder.

"Damn," he said out loud. He could see Berry riding out after him. Maybe the old fart is going out to join the boy, he thought. Whatever Berry was up to, Jo Jo knew that if he was going to get a gun from one of the hands, he would have to reach them ahead of Berry. He kicked his horse hard in the sides and raced ahead. He would ride it to death if he had to. He could get another horse as well as a gun from the hands.

• • •

Berry rode not as hard as Jo Jo, for he had more sense than his former foreman, and he had no intention of riding a horse to death. He also figured that he had time to reach the crew before they attacked the trail drivers and scattered the herd. He had specifically told them to wait at the mesa, and he did not think that the herd would actually reach the mesa until sometime the next day.

He felt confident that he would get there in plenty of time and that he would bring an end to the range war he had started. So far no one had been killed. No one had been hurt too badly either, and it was still possible, he told himself, to get his daughter back.

He thought that she was in love with Starkey. He had no way of knowing how Starkey felt about her, but he had no doubt that Brandy could get her man if she really wanted him. Well, they could get married, and eventually the two of them would own the whole damn valley after all. Berry told himself that would be enough. That would satisfy him. After all, what did a man build an empire for anyhow if not for his children? Yes, he thought, everything would be all right. He felt good. For the first time in years, he felt good about himself and about his relationship with Brandy.

Jo Jo found the Berry crew hidden in the shadows around the mesa. They were in a perfect spot for an ambush on the trail drivers, and the herd was not yet in sight. Well, Jo Jo didn't give a shit about any of that anymore. Let Starkey have his damn cows. Jo Jo had a new target. Two new targets. Berry and Berry's daughter. Besides, Starkey was sweet on Brandy, and what Jo Jo was planning to do to her would be plenty of revenge on Starkey. He rode the tired horse up to where the crew waited and dismounted.

"Jo Jo," said one of the hands. "Something wrong? You damn near rode that horse to death."

"Yeah," said Jo Jo. "We got a problem back at the ranch. I need your horse and gun."

"You need some help?"

"No. You all stay here and do what you were told. I can handle this other problem by myself. Just give me your horse and gun. Hurry up."

The gunslinger unbuckled his gun belt and handed it to Jo Jo, who took it and buckled it around his own waist. He moved to the side of the man's horse and took up the reins. As he swung into the saddle, he noticed a Winchester slung on the side of the saddle.

"I'll take this rifle too," he said.

"Well, what do you want me to do?" said the other.

"Like I said, just stay here and do what you was going to do," Jo Jo said. "I can take care of this other thing."

As Jo Jo rode away, the hand whose horse and guns were gone looked back toward the others.

"I wonder what the hell that was all about?" he said.

Jo Jo rode hard again, but this time he was not going to ride so far as before. He also rode more cautiously, for he did not want to come upon Berry unexpectedly. He knew that his only chance against his ex-boss was total surprise, and Berry had sworn to kill him on sight. He knew where he wanted to go, and he wanted to get back there before Berry reached the spot.

Soon he saw the clump of trees on the hillside just beside the trail. There was no sign yet of Berry, but Jo Jo knew that he would be along soon. He wasn't that far behind. He was probably riding easy, thinking that he had plenty of time. He wouldn't have figured Jo Jo for this kind of move. He thought that he was such a big man that when he ordered someone out of the territory he automatically got his way. Well, he'd find out different this time. He'd find out that no one orders Jo Jo Darby out of the country and gets away with it.

Jo Jo hid his horse well back of the trees, took the rifle out of the scabbard, and made his way through the thicket down to a spot near the trail. He settled himself in with a good view that would provide a straight shot. Everything was perfect. His only regret was that Berry would never know what had hit him, much less who it was that had done the deed.

He checked the load in the rifle, making sure that he had a bullet in the chamber. Then he took note of the sun. It was already low in the western sky. Berry had better be coming along soon, he told himself, or it would be dark. That might change the complexion of things. He began to feel nervous, and he noticed that his palms were starting to sweat. He wondered if he should forget it for this night and wait for a better time. He decided that he'd wait a little longer before he would allow panic to change his plans. If it got too dark for safety, so dark that he might miss with his first shot, he could always sit still and quiet and let Berry ride by.

Yes, he told himself, he'd stick. He'd wait and see. This was too good a setup to turn loose of, and he wanted Berry too bad to not take full advantage of it. It might even be better after dark. That way if someone else happened to come riding by, there would be less chance of their being able to identify the killer.

"Jo Jo," he said to himself, "calm down. Don't panic. Don't let it get to you. He's just a man, same as you. He takes his pants down to shit. And a bullet will stop him dead just the same as you or any other man."

14

Slocum was sitting on the porch of Starkey's house, watching the road. He didn't really expect any trouble from Berry's bunch that night, and he found his thoughts wandering to the pleasures of Veronica's bed. He stood up and walked into the house.

"Hey, boss," he said. "When are we heading out to meet the herd?"

"I told Panhandle we'd meet them at the mesa," said Starkey. "I reckon if we head out first thing in the morning, we'll get there just about right."

"First thing in the morning?" said Slocum.

"Yeah."

"You reckon you'll need me out here tonight?"

"Well, no, I can't think of any reason," said Starkey.

"Then if it's all right with you," said Slocum, "I think I'll take me a ride into town. You can pick me up on your way through."

"Sure," said Starkey. "Go ahead. I'll be leaving here about daybreak."

"I'll be waiting," said Slocum, and he headed out the door.

Jo Jo was about to give up, when he heard the sound of approaching hoofbeats. He quickly straightened himself up and leveled the rifle, ready for action. Nervous and sweating, he waited. Then he saw the horse and rider. His heart thrilled. He waited another moment until he was absolutely sure that he recognized his target. Then he took careful aim, and he squeezed the trigger.

Berry was feeling remarkably calm and satisfied in the knowledge that he was at last doing the right thing, and that good things would result from his actions. When the lead slammed into his chest, he died instantly, swayed in the saddle, and slowly slipped to the ground. There was a pleasant smile on his dead face.

Jo Jo whooped and ran down the slight incline to the trail and on over to the body. Nudging it with his foot, he flipped it over. Certain now of his success, he knelt and lay the rifle down on the ground. Then he went through the pockets, taking all the money he found and tossing everything else aside. He also took Berry's guns, a revolver and a rifle, and all of his extra ammunition.

"Hell," he said, "I should have done this a lot sooner. You ain't so tough now, you old son of a bitch, are you? Hell no. You ain't so tough now. Well, bye-bye, you bastard. Now I'm going to pay your little girl a visit. How do you like that? Can you hear me? God, I wish you could hear me."

Jo Jo did ride back to the ranch, but by the time he got there it was dark, and he wasn't at all sure that it would be safe for him to ride on up to the big house. Before riding out, Berry might well have told the cowboys there that he had fired Jo Jo, and he might even have set some guards around the house. Jo Jo decided to ride on into town for the remainder of the night and pay Brandy a visit during daylight hours. It would be much safer that way.

Slocum walked into the Dead Dog Saloon and found it as before—almost empty of customers. He didn't see Veronica either, but he went on inside and walked over to the bar.

"Kentucky bourbon," he said, tossing his money on the counter. "Leave the bottle."

He had tossed down the first drink and poured himself another, when the door to the back room was opened from the other side and Veronica stepped out. She stopped there in the doorway when she saw Slocum, and Slocum caught his breath. She was gorgeous. Of course, he knew that. That was why he had come to town. Still, he realized, he was never quite ready for the sight of her. She smiled.

"Hello, Johnny," she said. "And I had just about

convinced myself that it was going to be another one of those boring nights in Dead Dog.''

"I'm no guarantee," said Slocum.

Veronica walked on through the door, letting it shut behind her. She moved over to the bar directly across from Slocum and leaned her elbows on its edge, looking him in the face.

"You're a sight," he said.

"Is that good?" she asked.

"It's damn good."

"If it's that good," she said, "what's kept you away for so long?"

"I got a job," said Slocum. "We been busy."

"Yeah," Veronica said. "I've heard some things."

"Likely they're lies," said Slocum. He lifted his glass and sipped the brown whiskey. "Have some?" he asked.

"Don't mind if I do," said Veronica, and she reached under the bar for a glass. She put it on the bar and Slocum poured her a drink from his bottle. She lifted it and took a sip. "How long you in town for?" she asked.

Slocum smiled. "All night," he said.

"Merle," Veronica said, still staring at Slocum, "let's shut this place down as soon as those two cowboys over there are through with their drinks. You can lock the place up when you leave."

"Yes, ma'am," Merle said.

"You want to follow me upstairs?" she said to Slocum.

"Lady," said Slocum, "I'd follow you anywhere."

She led the way to the stairs and up to the room,

and Slocum followed with his bottle and glass. He reached around in front of her to open the door and then stood aside as she walked in. He followed, shut the door, and turned the key in the lock. She was standing beside the bed. Slocum crossed the room, put his bottle and glass on the bedside table, and took her in his arms.

She tilted her head back and let her lips part slightly, and Slocum bent to kiss her open, waiting, and wet mouth. As their lips met, she darted her tongue into his mouth, reaching around, searching, probing. Then gently she pushed away from him and reached to turn the bedclothes down for them. Then she stood up straight and began to slowly undress.

For a moment Slocum just stood and watched, fascinated to see each bit of flesh bared. First one shoulder, then the other. Then the firm breasts. He wanted to reach out immediately and get one in each hand, but he would have them soon enough. He started to shed his own clothes. Soon the two of them stood naked, facing each other, and there were two piles of clothing on the floor beside the bed.

Veronica's eyes roved down to Slocum's cock, by this time risen to about half its potential. She stepped forward and reached for it with both hands, wrapping one around the shaft and reaching under the heavy ball sack with the other. The eager cock responded almost immediately, growing and stiffening in her grip. She squeezed it hard and felt it throb.

Slocum put his hands on her smooth shoulders and turned her around so that she was facing the bed. Looking back over her shoulder at him, she leaned forward, resting her hands on the bed. Slocum stepped up close behind her. He put his hands on her magnificent round ass as she reached back between her legs to find his cock and guide it into her anxious cunt. Slocum shoved forward slowly, pushing himself all the way into her warm, wet channel, pressing his pelvis against her ass. She responded with a low moan and a wriggle of her ass. Then she arched her back, shoving herself back against him.

"Ah," she said. "Ah, that's good, Johnny. Now fuck me. Fuck me hard."

Slocum withdrew about halfway, then drove back in hard, slapping his pelvis against her ass, and he continued with a fast, hard rhythmic driving, giving her just what she asked for.

"Oh. Oh. Oh," she said as he slapped against her, driving in and out, in and out. At last he slowed, then stopped with his cock shoved all the way in. Veronica took advantage of his rest to wriggle her ass against him again, causing wonderful sensations inside her that thrilled throughout her body. Then Slocum started driving again.

"Oh, yes," she cried. "Oh. Oh. Oh."

She raised her legs one at a time to crawl up on the bed, resting on her hands and knees and shoving her ass more sharply into Slocum as he continued his hard driving. At last he stopped again, and this time he pulled out completely. His still-standing cock was gleaming from its soaking with her juices.

Veronica turned to lie back on the bed, but she did so from a sitting position, her ass still right at the edge. Then she lifted her legs and spread them wide, and Slocum, standing between them, saw her wide-open cunt, now sloppy-wet, waiting for his new attack. It didn't have to wait long.

He stepped in close and rammed his shaft in deep, leaning over her this time, resting his hands on either side of her on the bed. His face over hers, looking down on her, he was now driving downward, and she responded with upward thrusts of her pelvis. She reached up to put her hands on his shoulders.

Slocum slipped his hands underneath Veronica's back and lifted, and as he did so, he stood. Veronica realized what he was up to and did what she could to help by pulling herself up close to his by his shoulders. As Slocum stood straight, she wrapped her legs tight around his waist and her arms around his shoulders. Pressing her lips against his, she started to bounce herself up and down, riding his cock like a horse.

"Ahhh," said Slocum as he felt the pressure build down inside his balls. "Ah, here I come."

"Come then," Veronica shouted. "Shoot me full."

Then he spurted, burst after burst, shooting upward and into her already slippery wet tunnel. At last, spent, he carried Veronica to the bed and fell with her onto the mattress. For a long, quiet while they lay in each other's arms. Then she spoke softly into his ear.

"That was a wonderful fuck," she said. She kissed him on his lips.

"Yeah," he said. "It sure as hell was. The best, I'd say. Lady, if I was worth a shit, I'd settle down with you."

She lifted her head to look him in the eye.

"But you're not worth a shit," she said with a smile, "are you?"

"No," he said. "Not hardly. You know me pretty well, don't you?"

"I like to think so," she said.

Naked, they slept in each other's arms, a deep and satisfying sleep, and when they woke up sometime in the middle of the night, they fucked again, this time a long, slow, gentle fuck, and then they slept again.

Slocum woke up early the next morning and looked out the window to see the sun just beginning to show itself in the east. Starkey would be leaving the house just about now. Slocum intended to be ready to join him in his ride out to the mesa to meet the herd and to make sure that it got the rest of the way to the ranch in safety.

He dressed himself, then leaned over to wake Veronica with a kiss on the cheek. She opened her eyes with a smile and a soft moan of pleasure.

"I have to go," he said.

Slocum sat in a chair on the boardwalk in front of the Dead Dog Saloon. The chair was rocked back on two legs and leaned against the wall. His big 'Palouse waited patiently at the hitching rail, saddled and ready to go. Slocum smoked a cigar while he waited for Starkey to show. Out of the corner of his eye he noticed at the far end of the street, a man mounting a horse.

Casually he glanced that direction and recognized Jo Jo Darby. He saw that Jo Jo rode out of town in the direction of Berry's ranch, and he wondered if he was going there to organize the gunfighters for a raid on Starkey's herd. That would make sense.

Jo Jo was well out of town and out of sight by the time Starkey rode in. Starkey rode up beside Slocum's waiting stallion, and Slocum, still in his chair, looked up.

"About time," he said.

"Let's go, then," said Starkey.

Slocum dropped the chair forward and stood up.

"That Jo Jo fellow just rode out of here," he said. He nodded in the direction of Berry's ranch. "Going that way."

He stepped down into the street, unloosed the reins from the rail, and climbed into his saddle.

"Well, come on," he said, and they rode out of Dead Dog together, headed for the mesa.

15

"He could just be headed back for the ranch," said Slocum, "or he could be headed for your herd. I think we ought to get as close to him as we can, where we can watch where he goes."

"We give him time to get about halfway to Berry's place," said Starkey, "then we can hurry it up a little and catch up with him. From there he won't be able to see his back trail as well as the first half of the way."

They rode easily for a while, knowing that if they were to catch up with Jo Jo too quickly, while the road was fairly flat and straight, he'd be able to look back over his shoulder and see them. Slocum lit a cigar and smoked as they rode along.

He wondered if Jo Jo was going to the ranch to get

some of the Berry hands and ride out after Starkey's cows. That would be like Berry, judging from his past actions. Besides, if I were trying to run a man out, Slocum told himself, and if I knew that he had a herd coming in, I'd damn sure try to run them off.

He figured that Starkey's thoughts were on the same subject and were probably pretty much like his own. Since the mesa and the ranch were in the same direction along the same road from town, with the ranch being closer in there was no way for them to know where Jo Jo was headed until they reached the ranch to see whether he turned in or kept going. Or maybe he'd turn in and then round up the boys and head out again. They'd just have to wait and see.

Jo Jo was determined in his meanness, but he was also cautious. He had no idea what kind of orders Berry might have issued on the ranch before what turned out to be his final departure from that place. He might have told the cowboys to shoot Jo Jo on sight. He was certainly in the right mood for such an order.

And there was Brandy. She could shoot a rifle or a six-gun. Jo Jo had often seen her practicing, and he knew damned well that she could handle just about any kind of firearm. The approach to the ranch house was wide open. It could be difficult, if not impossible, to ride up there unseen.

He knew that he would make an attempt. More than that, he was confident that he would achieve his evil goal. He knew that he would get his hands on the girl and have his way with her. The only problem was just how and when to make his move. He sure didn't want to get in a hurry and ruin his chances.

He was a little better than halfway to the ranch from town, and the road had begun to wind and curve and climb up and down hills. The hillsides to the west of the road were covered with trees and thick brush. Jo Jo decided that he would move a little up the hillside when he reached the lane that turned into the ranch. He would hide up there for a little while and watch to see what was going on around the main house. When he was sure, he would make his move.

"Something's wrong here, Slocum," said Starkey. He halted his horse at the top of a rise, and Slocum pulled his stallion up beside him.

"What's wrong?" he said.

"We should have caught up with Jo Jo by now," Starkey said. "If he'd turned off to go to the ranch, we could see him from here. I think he's gone on ahead to the mesa, but why the hell would he go out there by himself?"

"Maybe he's already got some men out there," said Slocum. "Let's pick up our pace."

They rode faster then, on past the entrance to the Berry ranch, on toward the mesa and the glen where the cattle waited. They rode faster but still conscious of the length of time their mounts could stand the pace. They kept expecting to catch up with Jo Jo, but there was no sign of him ahead of them.

Suddenly Slocum spotted a riderless horse on the road ahead. His first thought was that the stupid Jo Jo might have fallen out of his saddle. He yelled at Starkey and pointed, and they rode up easy on the animal. Still saddled, it grazed contentedly along the side of the road. Slocum noticed the brand right away.

"It's one of Berry's," he said.

"It's not just one of Berry's," Starkey added. "It's his own personal horse. His favorite."

"Jo Jo wouldn't have been riding it?"

"No way," said Starkey. "I've never seen anyone on this horse but Ben Berry."

"Well," said Slocum, "we'd best look around."

They rode slowly then, looking carefully along each side of the road. It wasn't long before they found Berry. They recognized him at once. Both men dismounted to examine the body.

"Shot once," said Slocum. "I'd say a rifle shot. Likely from ambush, somewhere over there." He indicated the brushy hillside to the west. "Question is, if neither one of us done it, who did? And why?"

"One thing's almost for certain," said Starkey. "Whoever done it, we're almost for sure going to get blamed for it. Hell, if you was to have asked me who around these parts is most likely to shoot old Berry, I'd have named myself."

"Yeah," said Slocum. "Well, whoever it was, he robbed him. Took his guns and his money, it looks like. I'd say Berry was headed out to the mesa, and someone ambushed him."

"It couldn't have been any of Dusty's boys, do you think?" Starkey asked.

"I wouldn't think so," said Slocum.

"Just a road agent?"

"Not likely. But then, who knows? Anything's possible, I guess. Well, boss, what do we do now?"

Starkey wrinkled his face and scratched the side of his head. "Hell," he said, "it don't seem right to just leave him lying here—even if it is Berry. Let's catch up his horse, load him on it, and take him home."

"Why don't I do that," said Slocum. "You ride on out to your herd. Something might be happening out there."

"Yeah," Starkey agreed. "I'll help you with Berry. Then I'll head on out."

Jo Jo had been watching the ranch house for a while, and he had not seen much activity. He already knew, of course, that the gun hands were out at the mesa, waiting for Starkey's herd to show up. The cowhands, he figured, must be out on the range somewhere. It was, after all, a working cattle ranch. He decided that it was as good a time as any, and he would go ahead and make his move.

He mounted up and eased his way out of the thicket and down the side of the hill. At the edge of the road he hesitated, looked both ways, then rode across. He wasn't really worried about anyone except Berry's hands. He had seen Starkey and Slocum ride by earlier. Pretty soon, he figured, they would be shooting back and forth with the Berry gun hands. He found that thought amusing.

He rode onto the lane that would take him down to the big main ranch house and to Brandy. He licked his dry lips in anticipation, and he felt something move deep inside, deep down in his loins.

He tried to put those thoughts out of his mind.

There would be time enough later, he told himself. Just now he had to keep his mind on his own safety and on the success of his mission. As he rode, he moved his eyes from the big house to the area where the bunkhouse used to be. He was about halfway down the lane. He saw no movement. So far so good.

Back in Dead Dog, Hiram Dancer checked his weapons. He had put it off as long as he could, but he knew that Berry would be expecting him out at the mesa. He was a little miffed, because he didn't really think that he would be needed out there. In fact, he thought that it would make more sense for him to stay in town and conveniently not see anything. But Berry had been adamant about it. He wanted Dancer there.

There was going to be a showdown, he had said, once and for all. Starkey's cattle were going to show up, and Berry intended to scatter them all over the prairie. Starkey and Slocum would be there for sure, attempting to protect the herd, and so there would be a fight.

And Berry had said, "I want it to be the last fight. Do you understand me, Hiram?" And of course Dancer had said yes. He understood. He fastened the gun belt around his ample waist, picked up the rifle that was lying across his desk, and left the office.

As he walked down the street toward the livery stable, people took note. It wasn't often that they saw their sheriff carrying a rifle down the street. They watched as he went into the stable, and they waited while he waited as his horse was saddled for him.

Then, as the sheriff rode out of the stable and

headed out of town, they spoke to one another in amazement. "Where in the world is he going?" they asked each other, and no one had an answer to the question. They could not imagine what had motivated their indolent sheriff to ride out of town heavily armed. Finally someone said, "Maybe he's going rabbit hunting."

Riding toward the mesa, Starkey had a number of things on his mind. First, of course, was his new herd of cattle. With the mysterious disappearance of Jo Jo and then the discovery of Berry's body, he had no idea what to expect. He had thought that Berry's men would try to intercept the herd, but would they be out there without Berry or even Jo Jo? It didn't make sense.

But if the Berry bunch was out at the mesa without Berry or Jo Jo, but with orders to attack the herd, Dusty and his cowboys would have to fight. Starkey hated it that the cowboys who were just delivering his herd were about to be drawn into his fight. But then, he had warned them, and he had even offered to take over the herd from the mesa. He hoped that Berry's hands would either have the decency not to bring trouble on innocent bystanders, or better yet that they wouldn't have the stomach to start a fight without their boss.

Then he wondered if there might be an element to this conflict of which he was totally unaware, for someone had killed Ben Berry. Neither he nor Slocum was guilty of the deed. So who was? And what if anything did it have to do with his trouble with Berry?

And he thought about Brandy. She couldn't possibly know about the death of her father. If she had known, the body would not have been lying neglected on the road. Slocum would be informing her of the bad news, and it would be a shock to the poor girl. She would know about it only when she actually saw the body slung over a saddle.

He wondered what she would think. Would she believe that he had nothing to do with the murder? Probably not. She would blame him, almost for sure. Starkey himself could think of no one else likely to have killed Berry. Brandy was bound to think he had done it, and that would be the end of his relationship with Brandy.

No matter what she thought of Berry's actions, no matter what side she picked in the war, she could never love the man who was responsible for the death of her father, especially considering the way he had died. Shot from ambush. He never had a chance. It was a cowardly way to kill a man.

Back at the Berry ranch, Jo Jo was riding up to the house. He saw no one to oppose him. His heart pounded inside his chest in anticipation. He hoped that he would find Brandy inside. She must be there, he thought. Where else would she be? The front door of the house had not been repaired since the dynamite blast, and so there was not even that small barrier to slow him down.

He dismounted and looked around one more time. Still he saw no one watching him, no one even working around the corral or on the ruins of the bunkhouse.

He wrapped the reins of his horse around the hitching rail there in front of the big house, and he boldly stepped up onto the porch.

As eager as he was, he paused for a moment to look at the wreckage of the house he had once dreamed would one day be his own. He wondered for just an instant if there was yet some way to make that happen, but he quickly put that thought out of his mind. The dream was gone—all but one small part of it, and he was determined to live out that part.

He stepped up to the doorway, and his heart thrilled. He looked through into the large living room. The room was a mess. The furniture had all been shoved to the back of the room, away from the debris from the blast. He smirked. The Berrys deserved this mess, he thought. Puffed-up rich folks. They had lorded it over Jo Jo long enough. But those days were gone. He had left Ben Berry dead on the road, and now he was about to give Brandy just what she deserved.

16

Brandy was alone in her room upstairs in the big house. She had wanted to accompany her father to the mesa to call off the gun hands, but he had told her to wait for him at home. That had been the night before, and he had not returned. She was worried about him. She tried to imagine why he might have been out so long, and she could only think of two possible reasons. Neither was pleasant to contemplate.

Either he had changed his mind and decided to remain with the hands to attack Starkey's herd, or something had happened to him. Perhaps the fight had already started by the time he reached the mesa. She hoped for some possibility that had not yet entered her mind, but no matter how hard she thought about it, she couldn't come up with one.

She had just finished dressing in her riding clothes, and her intention was to ride out toward the mesa in spite of her father's wishes. She couldn't bear to just sit around the house and wait any longer. There might be trouble out there, but she could handle herself. She wasn't afraid of trouble.

On her way out of the house, she would pick up a six-gun and a rifle from the gun cabinet downstairs. She could handle either one, and she would if she had to. She pulled on her boots and stood up to leave the room. Then she heard the sound of footsteps downstairs, the sound of someone walking across the living room. She thought that it must be her father. She hoped that it was, and she hoped that he would tell her that everything was all right, and he would explain to her what it was that had delayed him for so long out there.

She rushed out of the room and down the hall to the top of the stairs, and then she stopped still, horrified. Down at the bottom step stood Jo Jo, and he was leering up at her. He had a hand on the banister and one foot on the first step. He was wearing a six-gun in a holster on his hip and another was tucked into the waistband of his trousers.

The last time she had seen him, he had been without a weapon of any kind. Her father had just taken his revolver away from him and ordered him off the ranch, threatening to kill him if he ever saw him again. Now here he was back on the ranch, in the house even, armed and grinning as if he hadn't a worry in the world. She wondered what it could mean, and she imagined the worst.

"What are you doing here?" she demanded of him.

"I come calling on you, pretty little missy," he said through his evil grin.

"Get out," she said.

Jo Jo climbed two steps. "Or what?" he said. "What are you going to do?"

"You've been ordered off this ranch," she said. "You have no right to be here."

Jo Jo continued his slow climb of the stairs, and the menacing grin stayed on his face. "I don't see no one around here who's going to do anything about it," he said. "Are you going to do anything about it? I know you can shoot, but I don't see no gun on you. The gun cabinet's downstairs, ain't it?"

"My father will kill you," she said.

"He ain't going to kill no one," Jo Jo said. "He ain't even going to threaten no one, not ever again. I done for him once and for all."

The horrible realization of what had happened hit Brandy like a shovel to the back of the head, but she didn't have time to cry or to grieve just then, and she knew it. She had to defend herself against Jo Jo. She knew what he wanted from her. He might intend to kill her eventually, but even if he did, she knew that he had other intentions for her before the killing. If she could help it, he wouldn't accomplish either of those goals.

She looked over her shoulder and thought about running, but there was really no place for her to go. The only way out from the upstairs was blocked by Jo Jo, and there were no weapons on the second floor. If she was going to escape him, she would have to get herself downstairs, and the only way down was right through him.

He kept coming. He didn't seem to be in a hurry. He was savoring the moment, enjoying being a menace. He took the steps slowly, one at a time. Brandy's thoughts were a rush in her head. She knew she had to do something. He came closer. Then she thought, what's the last thing he would expect me to do? And it came to her.

She ran down the stairs straight for him, and she ran screaming. He stopped, surprised, astonished. He had been expecting her to turn and run the other way. His eyes opened wide, and he lifted his hands to defend himself, but he was too late. She was practically on him, and she unleashed a right cross that caught him square on the jaw.

It was the last thing in the world he expected from her, the last thing he would have expected from any woman. It stunned him. It even frightened him a little, and it staggered him. He might have fallen down the stairs had he not been holding tight to the rail.

Brandy had taken him by surprise, but she knew that to really take advantage of her surprise attack, she had to keep moving. She couldn't allow him time to recover from his surprise and make his counterattack. Her right had caused him to turn to his right. He was gripping the rail with his right hand and leaning over it. As he started to straighten up, she reached, growling and snarling, for his eyes with both her hands.

"Ahh," he screamed, and covered his face with both hands, at the same time turning his back on her. She put a foot on his ass and shoved hard, and Jo Jo went flying down the stairs. He howled and cursed all the way, bumping his face and barking his knees and elbows on the steps as he landed. Brandy thought quickly, looked over the railing, and saw the big couch down there. It had been shoved back because of the hole in the front wall. She put a hand on the railing and vaulted over, landing hard on the couch. Jo Jo was up on his feet by this time, and he crouched low, ready to spring into action.

"You goddamned little bitch," he said. "I'll make you sorry for that."

"I'm already sorry I ever met you," Brandy snapped. "You cowardly little chicken shit."

She glanced across the room at the gun cabinet, and Jo Jo followed her glance.

"You can't get to that before I can," he said, and for the first time since his tumble, the grin returned to his face. "You might just as well come along with me and save us both some trouble, 'cause I'm going to get you in the end."

"I'd as soon couple with a cur dog as with you," she said. "You make me puke."

She edged a little toward the gun cabinet, and Jo Jo edged a little that way in response. Then she ran, and he did too. Brandy reached the cabinet before Jo Jo, and she jerked open a drawer where the revolvers were kept, but before she could reach into the drawer to grab one, Jo Jo was there. He slammed the drawer shut, and she barely got her hand out of the way.

She reached up above the drawer for a rifle, and Jo Jo grabbed at her wrist. In their scuffle they knocked the rifles out of the cabinet. Jo Jo slapped at the falling rifles, and while he was thus distracted, Brandy reached for the six-gun that was tucked in his waistband. She pulled it loose, but he grabbed her wrist and held it in his left hand, and with his right he slapped her hard across the face.

"Take that, bitch," he said. "Stuck-up bitch."

He slapped her again and again. She thumbed back the hammer on the six-gun and pulled the trigger, firing a shot that went past Jo Jo's left thigh into the living room floor. He yelped, and she thumbed back the hammer again. Then Jo Jo turned all his attention to the gun in her hand, trying now with both his hands to wrench it loose from her grip.

She pulled the trigger again, but the web between the thumb and forefinger of his right hand was caught beneath the cocked hammer, and when it fell, it snapped on his loose flesh. He screamed and jerked his hand, tearing the skin. His other hand still gripped Brandy by the wrist. He put the palm of his wounded but free hand against her face and pushed her to the wall, at the same time wrenching the revolver loose from her grip.

Then he pressed his body against hers, pushing her even harder against the wall, and he mashed his slobbering open lips against her mouth. She twisted her face, attempting to escape his loathsome kiss, and she spat, but he kept pressing. Two cowboys stepped into the living room through the open front door just then. Neither was armed.

"Hey," one of them shouted.

Jo Jo turned and fired, and the puncher dropped. The other hesitated. Jo Jo pointed his revolver at the man. He tried to think what to do. The others might also be back. Obviously he was not going to get his way here and now. He would have to take Brandy away with him, and he had only the one horse saddled and waiting in front of the house.

"You going to kill me too?" the cowboy asked.

"You do just what I say," Jo Jo said, "and I'll let you live." He grabbed Brandy hard by the wrist and headed for the door, pulling her after him. "Walk ahead of me," he said to the cowboy, "but go slow."

The cowboy went out the doorway, and Jo Jo, pulling Brandy along, followed. When the cowboy was alongside Jo Jo's mount, Jo Jo stopped him.

"Climb up on that horse," he told Brandy, "and put your hands on the saddle horn."

She did as he said, and he jerked a short piece of rope loose from the saddle and held it out toward the cowboy.

"Take this and tie her hands to the horn," he said, "and make a good job of it."

The cowboy looked up at Brandy.

"Go ahead," she said. "Do what he says."

"That's good advice," said Jo Jo. "Now do it."

The cowboy tied Brandy's hands to the saddle horn, and Jo Jo untied the reins from the hitching rail so he could lead the horse.

"Now," he said, "we're going over to the corral, and you're going to saddle me up another horse."

Moving toward the corral, Jo Jo looked nervously around, but he saw no more cowboys. If he could get out of there fast enough, he thought, he would still be all right. The cowboy caught a horse and threw a saddle on it. Jo Jo swung up onto the horse's back, still holding the reins to Brandy's mount. Then he swung the barrel of the revolver around and shot the cowboy in the chest.

"Damn," said Brandy. "You didn't have to do that."

"I don't like to have no witnesses," said Jo Jo. "Besides, you ought to be worrying about your own self, not no damn two-bit cowhand."

He kicked his new mount in the sides and turned it toward the lane that would lead him off the ranch, pulling the other horse along behind him.

"You little rat shit," Brandy yelled at Jo Jo's back.

He turned in the saddle and pointed the revolver at her. "Listen, bitch," he said, "I plan for you and me to have a little fun, but if you piss me off too much, I'll kill you here and now. You understand me?"

"I understand you," she said, "but I'd just as soon you shoot me now and get it over with."

Jo Jo grinned again. "Don't you wish," he said. Then he turned again and started riding hard toward the road. At the end of the lane he turned, not toward the mesa, but toward town. Brandy wondered where he might be taking her. He must be planning to turn off somewhere, for he couldn't possibly be stupid enough to ride into town with her like this.

It was clear to her, though, that he did not want to chance running into any of the Berry hands or Starkey and Slocum. For that reason, obviously, he had turned the other way. She wondered how much time she might have before he decided to stop somewhere with her, and she wondered what kind of chance she would have against him this time.

He would have to untie her hands in order to get her down out of the saddle. That might be her best opportunity. She tried to think it through. If he was on the ground and reached up to untie her hands, she could let him get the job done, then kick the horse into a run. She might just get away from him. He could either remount his horse and give chase, or he could take a shot at her as she rode away. She decided that would be her ploy, and she thought it through again and again. When the time came, she wanted to be ready. One thing was for damn sure. That sorry bastard Jo Jo was not going to have his way with her without a hell of a fight. She would see to that.

17

Slocum reached the lane that wound its way down to the Berry ranch house, and he turned down it, leading his unhappy load. He was not looking forward to his present chore. At best, he had to inform a young woman of the death of her father by the hand of some unknown murderer. At worst, the young woman might accuse him or his boss of the murder. If any of Berry's gun hands were around, there could be trouble, and Slocum would be right in the middle of it. Any way you looked at it, it was not a pleasant task.

But it had to be done, and Starkey was on his way to meet Dusty and Panhandle and the other cowboys who were bringing in his herd. If the gun hands were not on the ranch, they would probably be out at the mesa waiting for the herd to arrive, and if they were out there, there would be no question about it—there would be trouble, and Starkey would be the one in the middle.

Given the circumstances, they had a choice. They had to split up. Someone had to go ahead and meet the herd, and someone had to take Berry's body home. Slocum figured that after he had delivered the body and the bad news, he would be able to afford to ride his stallion a little harder. The ride to the ranch had been slow-paced.

He was about halfway down the lane toward the ranch house when Hiram Dancer rode past back on the road going toward the mesa. He did not see Dancer, nor had Dancer seen him.

Starkey reached the mesa without seeing anyone else on the road, and he did not immediately see the herd of cattle. They must have been moving a little more slowly than he expected, so he continued on his way to meet them. He was well beyond the mesa when he saw the dust of the herd. Panhandle saw him coming and rode ahead to meet him.

"Howdy, Mr. Starkey," he yelled as he came closer.

"Howdy, Panhandle," said Starkey. "Everything still in good shape?"

"Everything's just fine."

"No sign of trouble?"

"Not so far. Come on back and meet Dusty and the rest of the boys."

They rode together back toward the approaching

cattle. Panhandle waved his wide-brimmed hat over his head, and another rider responded. When they met, Panhandle introduced Starkey to Dusty. The lowing of the cattle filled the air, and the men had to talk loud to be heard.

"They look good," Starkey said.

"We've took it pretty easy on them," Dusty said. "Even so, I think we'll still have to bed them down when we reach the mesa there, close as we are. We can take them on into your place in the morning. If that's all right with you."

"Sure," said Starkey. "Whatever you think."

Dusty looked over his shoulder and yelled, "Keep them moving, boys. Let's go."

"Dusty," said Starkey, "did Panhandle tell you about the trouble I'm expecting?"

"He told me," said Dusty, "and I told all the boys. We've been watching all sides pretty close."

"I told him that I'd take over from here," said Starkey. "The trouble ain't yours, and I sure didn't pay you to fight, just to drive cows."

"And did he tell you that when I promise to deliver cows, I deliver them?" Dusty said.

"Well, yeah," said Starkey.

"Enough said, then."

Dusty turned his horse and raced after a cow that wandered out of the herd, and Panhandle eased up beside Starkey.

"What'd I tell you, Pard?" he said.

Starkey shrugged. "Let's drive these cows," he said.

• • •

Hiram Dancer rode puffing up to the shadow at the base of the mesa and joined the gang of gunslingers there. The dust of the approaching herd of cattle had just come into their view.

"Sheriff," said one of the gunnies, "we didn't know you was coming out here today."

"Hell," said Dancer, "I didn't intend to, but Berry insisted. I see that herd's coming up on us."

"Yeah. They'll likely try to bed them down right below in that pasture."

"I don't reckon any of them will get much sleep," Dancer said. "Cows or cowboys. And, boys, I don't think Mr. Berry would mind at all if young Mr. Starkey didn't live through the night."

"Where is Mr. Berry, Sheriff? He told us he'd be here. We ain't supposed to do nothing without he gives the word first."

"I reckon he'll show," said Dancer. "We'll just hang tight here."

Slocum had almost reached the big house, when he saw the man on the ground over by the corral. He rode over there instead and dismounted. He could see the blood on the man's shirtfront, and he could also see that the man was still alive. He knelt and lifted the man's head.

"Hey, partner," he said. "You've been hit pretty hard."

"Jo Jo," the man whispered.

"He shot you?" Slocum asked.

"Shot me," said the man. "Took Miss Brandy and rode out toward town."

"Damn," said Slocum. "Well, I can't leave you here like this. Can you make it to the house if I help you?"

"I don't know. I'll try."

Slocum was helping the man up, when four cowboys came riding in. "What's going on here?" one of them demanded.

"This man's hurt," said Slocum. "Take care of him."

The cowboy who had spoken pulled a revolver and leveled it at Slocum. The others followed his lead.

"We'll take care of him all right," said the leader, "but you ain't going no place till we find out what happened here."

The wounded man then spoke up in a harsh whisper. "Jo Jo shot me," he said. "Not him. Jo Jo. Let him go."

The cowboys looked at one another, then holstered their guns and dismounted to tend to their fallen comrade. Slocum mounted his stallion quickly. As he rode away, he said over his shoulder, "Your boss has been killed too. I brought him back."

This time he rode hard. At the end of the lane he turned toward town. He figured that Jo Jo couldn't be too far ahead of him. He knew what time Jo Jo had ridden out of town that morning and about what time it had been when he had arrived at the ranch. Slocum and Starkey had gone on a little farther and discovered Berry's body. Then Slocum had gone back to the ranch. No, he told himself. Jo Jo can't be too far ahead.

He wondered if he should slow down and be more

careful, but he nixed that thought. There was no telling what that slimy Jo Jo bastard was up to, and Slocum felt that it was urgent he catch up with them. Besides, he told himself, he could handle Jo Jo even if Jo Jo surprised him. Even so, he recalled Berry's body, shot from ambush, and it suddenly seemed likely that Jo Jo had done that deed.

There was no question he had shot the Berry cowhand back at the ranch and carried off Brandy. Those actions seemed to clear up the murder of Berry too. They also clearly indicated that Jo Jo was not above laying an ambush· and shooting his victim without warning. Slocum's advantage, if he had one, was that Jo Jo did not know that he was in pursuit.

But where the hell, he wondered, could Jo Jo be taking Brandy? Even he could not be stupid enough to ride with her into town. So what was there between the ranch and town? There was almost no cover in terms of woods. That kind of cover was all in the other direction, between the Berry ranch and the mesa.

Then he remembered having seen an old line shack along the way. It was only a mile or two out of town, on Berry's property, and it would be on Slocum's left as he rode toward town. There was a little creek there, and a small stand of trees. The shack was backed up against the trees. That was a possibility.

Jo Jo rode hard into the trees behind the shack, still leading the other horse by its reins. In the cover of the trees he stopped and dismounted. He slapped the reins of both horses around low branches, then he reached up to untie Brandy's hands from the saddle horn. He hesitated, realizing the situation he had put himself in.

He was standing on the ground, and both his hands would be occupied in the untying. She was in the saddle still. He knew her well enough to know that she would try something, and she would never have a better chance. He decided that he would have to be ready for her. His advantage was that the horse was tied to the branch, and that it would be difficult to maneuver the animal in the close woods.

He looked up at her and she glared back down at him. He grinned and reached up to untie her hands.

"It won't be long now," he said. "Hell, you might like it so much that you'll decide you want to stick with me."

"There's about as much chance of that as a laying hen flying to the moon," she said. Jo Jo busied himself with the rope. "If you don't kill me first," she said, "I'll kill you. And that's a promise."

Jo Jo jerked the rope loose.

"Shut up," he snapped.

Brandy kicked the horse in the sides and yelled to get it going, but it shied and reared, and Jo Jo reached up, taking her around the waist and pulling her out of the saddle. She kicked and struggled as he dragged her out of the woods and into the shack. Inside, he flung her hard onto the floor. She scooted a bit and scampered to her feet, coming up in a crouch ready to do battle, but Jo Jo had pulled a revolver and was holding it pointed at her midsection.

"I'll gut-shoot you," he said. "I don't want to. At least not yet, but I will. I damn sure will."

Brandy stood still.

"That's more like it," said Jo Jo. "Now you can just start taking off them clothes. I've waited a long time for this."

"I won't do it," Brandy said. "Go ahead and shoot."

"If I shoot," said Jo Jo, "I won't kill you. I'll just hurt you, and then I'll get what I want anyway. Now, you do what I say. Take off that shirt and let me see them tits."

Brandy hesitated, and Jo Jo fired a shot that went close by her head and made her ears ring. She flinched.

"Get to it," Jo Jo roared.

Brandy's fingers trembled as she reached for the top button on her blouse. She fumbled a moment.

"Come on," said Jo Jo. "Hurry it up."

She got the first button undone and reached for the second one. She tried to think of ways to get out of the situation she was in. Even in the small shack there was too much distance between the two of them for her to get away with rushing him. He would get off a shot before she could reach him.

Maybe he wouldn't have time to avoid killing her, but if he did manage to only wound her, she had no doubt that he would do as he had threatened. He would crawl all over her and rape her as she lay bleeding to death. And if she didn't continue to undress, he would shoot her anyway. She hated the thought, but maybe her only chance was to take off her clothes. Then he would have to come close to accomplish his purpose, and perhaps she could attack him some way.

Get his eyes or his balls. Something. She undid a third button.

"Hurry it up," said Jo Jo, and just then they heard the unmistakable sound of pounding hooves. Jo Jo backed to the door, still holding the six-gun on Brandy. Brandy stood still, her heart pounding with anticipation. At the door Jo Jo looked back over his shoulder, and he saw Slocum riding toward the shack.

"Damn," he said. "Dammit. Dammit."

He had to stop Slocum, but he was afraid to turn his back on Brandy. He suddenly felt himself to be in a desperate situation. He thought about the rifle in the saddle boot out in the woods. He turned back toward Brandy and motioned with the barrel of his revolver.

"Come on," he said. "Outside."

Brandy walked across the room and out the door.

"On back to the horses," he said, and she walked into the trees. "Lay down," said Jo Jo. "Now. Get down on your belly."

Brandy did as Jo Jo said, and Jo Jo holstered his six-gun and drew the rifle out of the boot. Brandy was on the ground in front of him. He leaned against a tree trunk and lined up his shot. Slocum was moving along at a good clip, not leisurely the way Berry had been. He'd have to be careful. He sighted in and followed his target for a bit. Then he pulled the trigger.

The rifle boomed, and off in the distance Slocum's hands went to his head, and he fell off the backside of his horse.

"I got him," said Jo Jo gleefully. "I got the son of a bitch. Get up."

Brandy stood slowly, and Jo Jo grabbed her by an arm.

"Get mounted," he said. "We're getting out of here."

18

Everything was black and swimming, and in the blackness was a host of little stars moving about like fireflies and sometimes like skyrockets on the Fourth of July. And there was pain, intense pain, pain like the worst hangover of all time. He was not unconscious. That would have been merciful. He was very conscious, aware of a sharp pain and a flash of light in his head, aware of falling and of landing with a hard thud, aware of the world swirling around him in darkness, and aware of the pain.

He rolled on the ground and moaned, and he squeezed his eyes tight, trying to clear his vision. He opened his eyes, blinked a few times, then left them open. The thick blackness was gone and he could see the sky overhead, but the world was still spinning.

Slowly he sat up, and his left hand went to his head almost automatically. He winced when he touched the spot, and he brought his hand down in front of his eyes and looked at the blood.

Things slowly came clear to him. He had been in pursuit of that damned Jo Jo, who had kidnapped Brandy, and he had headed for the line shack, thinking that it might be a likely place for Jo Jo to have taken her. Then came the explosion in his head. The little shit shot me, he said to himself. Just the way Berry got it. Shot from ambush. No warning.

He reached up to feel the wound on his head again, this time carefully and consciously. The shot had grazed his head. Another inch or two and he'd be lying dead, his brains scattered on the prairie. Hell, he told himself, you survive any way you can. Sometimes by skill. Sometimes by luck. What matters is that you survive.

With a tremendous effort he got himself to his feet, and he staggered a step or two. Then he stood still, yet he was swaying. He looked around for his 'Palouse, and saw it, waiting patiently for him to come around. He took a deep breath and tried to clear his head.

Then he walked with uneasy steps over to the big stallion. He put his hands on the saddle to steady himself, and he just stood there for a moment. Finally, he lifted a foot to a stirrup and swung himself up into the saddle. He settled with a loud groan. He felt for the Colt at his side. It was there. The Winchester was in the saddle boot, where it belonged.

That stupid Jo Jo had dropped him and then run,

not bothering to make sure of his victim. Well, Slocum told himself, the little shit would live just long enough to regret that foolish mistake. He decided that he had allowed himself enough time to recover, and he turned the 'Palouse and headed for the shack.

He had not seen any horses on his initial approach, so he knew that they must have been hidden in the trees. He rode in, looking for a sign. If Jo Jo had panicked as Slocum figured, he would not have gone back to the road. He looked for sign of horses heading cross country, and soon he found it. Two horses had moved out of the small stand of trees and headed directly across the Berry ranch.

Slocum looked after them. The open, flat country didn't last long in that direction. It gave way to rolling hills, and obviously Slocum had been out of commission long enough for the riders to have reached those hills. He started after them.

Brandy's hands were no longer tied to the saddle horn. Jo Jo had been in too much of a hurry to retie the rope, but he did hold the reins to her mount as before. As far as she knew, no one was following them. No one knew where she was or what had happened to her. She was on her own. She was getting farther away from the possibility of any help, yet, she told herself, she was better off than she had been before. Her hands were free.

Jo Jo was lashing furiously at his poor horse, driving it as hard as he dared over the hills. The ground was getting rocky underfoot and more precarious. He knew, of course, that he should be more careful, but he was in a hurry to get some distance between himself and the Berry ranch. Something in his head told him that he was overreacting, that he had killed Berry and Slocum, and no one would be in pursuit.

But then, he had thought himself safe at the ranch house and again at the shack, and he had been surprised at both places. The cowhands all probably knew about him by this time, and they might have also informed the gunslingers. On the other side were Starkey and the cowboys who had brought in his herd. He wanted to get far away from them all.

He had made a serious mistake, and he was aware of it now. He had been eager to unleash his lust on Brandy. Had he just taken her at the ranch house and led her away to a safe place, he would have been all right. He had wasted time at the ranch house and again at the shack, and because of that his trail had been followed.

Well, he wouldn't make that mistake again. He had Brandy. He could afford to take the time now to get her away to some place safe, somewhere away from the Berry ranch and Starkey and all of them. And when he arrived at that safe place, he told himself, he would show her a thing or two.

Jo Jo topped a rise and suddenly found himself faced with a steep and rocky descent on the other side. He had to slow the pace to allow the horses to pick their way down the hillside. It was slow going and a bit chancy, especially with Jo Jo holding the reins to Brandy's horse, but he sure didn't want to let her loose. They slipped a time or two, but they made it safely to the bottom.

Then Jo Jo realized that he had ridden into a small valley with no way out again but up the side of the next hill, one very much like the one he had just come down. He looked around, desperately seeking an easier way out of the hole, but he could see none. He urged his tired horse forward.

"Come on," he said. "Come on."

The valiant horse tried. It started up the slippery hillside, but its front hooves slipped on loose rocks, and Jo Jo was tossed forward. He clutched at the saddle horn and managed to keep his seat, but in doing so he lost his hold on the reins to Brandy's mount. Brandy saw her chance.

Leaning forward, practically lying on the horse's neck, she stretched her arm to gather up the loose reins. She had them. Jo Jo was still fighting to regain control of his own disoriented mount.

Brandy's horse, having been led by Jo Jo, was not as far up the side of the hill as was his. She backed it down quickly. There was no easy escape, but she rode a distance away from Jo Jo on the valley floor. She looked around for another up the side, any side. It looked about as rough one way as another. She decided that the way they had come down was as good as any.

She turned the horse and started back up the very trail they had broken only a moment before. Just about then, Jo Jo's horse fell over on its side, and Jo Jo just barely managed to get his leg out from under the heavy beast. He was on his back, sliding down the hillside headfirst and screaming all the way. To his right, very near, the horse slid, struggling all the while to get back to its feet.

On the floor, Jo Jo scrambled to his feet. His trousers were torn and his knees were skinned and bloody. He looked at his horse, still trying to get to its feet, but by now down at the bottom of the hill. Then he turned and looked at Brandy, halfway up the other hill and about to make good her escape from him.

"Shit," he said. "Damn."

He looked back at the horse. It struggled to its feet. He hurried to its side and gathered the reins. Grabbing the saddle horn, he tried to mount, but the animal was fidgeting nervously.

"Stand still," he shouted. "Damn you."

As the horse moved, Jo Jo danced on one foot, trying to get himself up on its back. He managed to glance over his shoulder at Brandy. She was nearing the top.

"You come back down here," he shouted, but he was still dancing around his nervous horse. "Come back, you bitch."

As her horse's front hooves reached for the top edge, Jo Jo lost his balance and fell hard on his back. It was a painful fall onto the hard, jagged rocks, but he fell so that he was looking up toward Brandy. He winced as he pulled out his revolver.

"I'll kill you," he shouted.

Brandy and her horse went over the edge just as Jo Jo snapped off a wild shot. Then she disappeared from his view.

"Dammit. Dammit. Dammit," he shouted. He ran after his horse, which was still frightened and still

stamping around, trying to figure out what it was going to do. Jo Jo's demeanor didn't help matters at all.
It flinched away from him as he reached for it. He
realized that he needed both hands, so he reluctantly
shoved the revolver back into the holster at his side.

He ran toward the horse. It shied and ran away from
him. He ran after it, and it ran past him. As it did he
reached for it and nearly fell over again. He looked
up the walls of the hole he was in, and he knew that
he was in deep shit if he could not manage to get back
on the horse.

Back up on top of the hill, Brandy found the going
once again easier. It was still not smooth enough to
race blindly ahead, and she knew that the horse under
her was tired. She rode down the hillside and up the
next rather easy rise, and then she saw Slocum coming
in her direction. She was startled, for she had thought
that Jo Jo had killed him. She urged the horse forward
a little faster until she met him.

"Thank God," she said. "I thought you were
dead."

"Are you all right?" Slocum asked.

"Yeah," she said. "I'm fine now."

"Where's Jo Jo?"

Brandy pointed back behind her.

"Over the second hill back," she said. "It's a steep
and rocky drop down into a rat trap. The last I saw
him, he was unhorsed down there."

Slocum thought about the possible trouble Starkey
was in, but he decided that he would not let Jo Jo get
away. He would take care of that sorry little bastard

first, then ride to the mesa. He moved his big stallion forward, and Brandy moved alongside him.

Soon they found themselves at the top of the steep hillside, looking down into the hole. Jo Jo had given up the struggle with his horse, at least for a time. He was sitting, dejected, on a rock. The horse stood a safe distance away from him, watching him. Neither seemed to have noticed the arrival of the two riders at the top of the hill. Slocum dismounted and stepped up close to the edge.

"Jo Jo," he said.

Jo Jo whirled and looked up to see Slocum standing there.

"You," he said, astonished. "I shot you."

"Well, I ain't dead," said Slocum. "But you will be, real soon."

Jo Jo stood up and slapped leather at the same time. Slocum pulled out his Colt and sent a bullet into Jo Jo's chest. Jo Jo's revolver had only just cleared leather. He stood stupidly, knees bent, the gun pointed at the ground just in front of him. He was looking down at the new hole in his chest.

"Die, damn you," Brandy shouted.

Jo Jo rolled his eyes up toward Brandy. He stood for a moment, swaying and staring at her. Then he pitched forward onto the rocks dead.

"Mr. Slocum," Brandy said, "that may have been the best thing you ever did in your life."

"Yes, ma'am," Slocum said. "And now I have to give you the worst news I've ever had to deliver. Me and Starkey found your father on the road. He's dead, ma'am. Shot from ambush. I'm sorry."

Brandy looked down at the body of the hated Jo Jo Darby.

"I know," she said. "Jo Jo did it. He admitted it to me. No. It was more like he bragged about it. Damn his soul to hell. I wish I could kill him again."

"I brought the body into the ranch house," Slocum said.

"Well, what are you doing here?" Brandy asked.

"A cowboy at the corral told me what had happened. He'd been shot."

"Slim," said Brandy. "He's alive?"

"I think he'll be all right," said Slocum.

"Thank God," Brandy said once again. "But you said that you and Sammy found my father."

"That's right," said Slocum. "We were on our way out to meet his cattle, and we found him on the road there. We were afraid that there might be some trouble out there, so we decided that he should go on, and I'd bring your father home."

"I thank you for that," said Brandy. She glanced back down at Jo Jo. "And for this." Then she remembered why her father had been riding to the mesa. "But we'd better get on back to Sammy," she said. "He might need some help out there."

"Let's get that poor horse out of that hole first," said Slocum. "We can't leave him down there like that."

"Well, all right," she said, "but let's hurry it up."

19

Slocum and Brandy rode slowly for a while, even though they both felt that their mission was urgent. But both horses had been ridden hard, and they wanted to make sure that they reached their goal without killing a horse and having to walk the rest of the way. As they rode, she told him that she knew that her father had sent gunmen to the mesa to ambush the cowboys and scatter the herd. She knew it because he had told her.

"But he was on his way out there to stop them," she said. "He would have too if that damned Jo Jo hadn't—"

Her voice quavered just a bit toward the end, and she stopped talking.

"If you don't mind me asking," said Slocum,

"what was it made Mr. Berry change his mind? He seemed pretty dead set on getting Starkey out of the valley."

"He was," Brandy admitted. "He was stubborn as hell about it. I had more than one argument with him on the subject. In fact, I was so mad at him that I was going to leave home."

Slocum shot a questioning look at Brandy.

"I was," she said. "Oh, I know what you're thinking. I'm a pampered, spoiled brat, and I wouldn't know what to do with myself away from home. Well, I was scared, but I was leaving."

"Why didn't you?" Slocum asked.

"Jo Jo happened along, and he attacked me. I was fighting with him when Daddy came up. He threw Jo Jo on the ground, disarmed him, and fired him. He told him if he ever saw him again, he'd kill him."

"That explains a lot of things," said Slocum.

"Yeah. I guess that seeing—like that—what kind of men he was using to get what he wanted—well, I don't know. I guess it made him think about what kind of man he'd become. He told me about the ambush, and he said that he'd go out there and stop it. He said the war was over."

"But that Jo Jo lurked around to get his revenge," said Slocum, "first on your daddy and then on you."

"He might have too," said Brandy, "if you hadn't come along."

"I wish I'd killed him sooner," said Slocum.

"Well, I'm grateful to you," she said. "I always will be."

"Forget it," said Slocum. "I'm just working for wages."

He felt like he was getting his first real introduction to this young woman, and he could see now why Starkey was so hung up on her. He glanced over at her. She was beautiful, and she was bold. Hell, he thought, he could go for her himself if—

"You know," he said, "if Sam Starkey doesn't marry you, he's a damn fool. I think we can hurry these horses along a little now."

Starkey was riding between Dusty and Panhandle alongside the herd, and the mesa was looming ahead.

"Dusty," he said, "if there's going to any trouble along the way, it'll come at us just ahead. There's lots of places to hide at the base of that mesa."

"Panhandle," Dusty said, "pass the word around to the boys to be on the lookout."

"Yes, sir," said Panhandle, and he turned his mount to ride back toward the cowboys at the rear of the herd.

"You think they'll hit us?" Dusty asked.

"My best guess is that they will," said Starkey. "I'd sure as hell like to be wrong." He squinted, straining to see into the distance ahead. "Dammit," he said. "I wish Slocum was here."

"Slocum?" said Dusty. "Would that be John Slocum?"

"Yeah. You know him?"

"Hell yes. I seen him in action too," said Dusty. "Is he with you?"

"He's working for me," said Starkey.

"Well, by God," Dusty said, "if there's trouble up ahead, I agree with you one hundred percent. I wish to hell Slocum was here."

In the shadows at the base of the mesa, Sheriff Hiram Dancer and the Berry gunmen watched the approach of the Starkey herd. It would soon be within striking distance.

"What're we going to do?" one of the gunnies asked Dancer.

Dancer wiped the sweat from his brow with a sleeve. He didn't like this kind of work, and it pissed him off that Berry had made him join in. He didn't relish the idea of attacking a bunch of cowboys he didn't even know without the boss being right there beside him giving the orders. But, he asked himself, what if Berry's testing me? What if I let them go by just because he's not here? What'll he say about that?

Dancer knew that Berry wanted the herd scattered, and Berry had made a special point of telling Dancer to be there. Now Berry had failed to show. Did he want Dancer to take over and see the job through? It seemed likely. Dancer had nothing he believed in to pray to, but had he been a praying man, he would have been praying that Berry show up in the nick of time to save him from having to make this painful decision on his own.

The herd was getting closer and closer. Who the hell would think a damn herd of cows would move along so fast? he asked himself. Then, all of a sudden it seemed, they were too close. It was time to make a move. He had to decide.

"Mount up, boys," he said. "Get ready to hit them."

He lumbered up into his saddle and the others did likewise. He pulled out his revolver, and they all did the same. He urged his horse forward, and the others followed him. They rode in a bunch out of the cover of the shadow, and they stopped, posing a menace to the cowboys driving the herd along.

"There they are," said Dusty.

"Yeah," said Starkey. "It looks like a fight for sure."

Dusty turned in the saddle and waved his big hat to Panhandle, who came riding up beside his boss. "Get the boys all up here together," he said.

"You don't want to leave no one to watch the cows?" Panhandle asked.

"Nope. Get them up here."

"If there's shooting," said Panhandle, "we'll lose them."

"If we get out of this alive," Dusty said, "we can gather them up again. We need every gun we can get right up here. Now, get moving."

"Yes, sir," said Panhandle, and he turned to ride off again.

"What's it look like to you?" Dusty asked Starkey.

"About an even fight," Starkey answered.

"Yeah," said Dusty.

"They're all professional gunfighters though," Starkey added. "Not just cowboys."

"Well, don't sell my boys short, pardner," Dusty said. "Those bastards'll damn sure know they've been in a fight. I can promise you that much.''

Slowly the cowboys gathered up around Dusty and Starkey, and two bunches of armed and mounted men faced one another across a short expanse of prairie. The small herd of cattle milled about behind the cowboys. Old Berry's dead, Starkey thought, but the son of a bitch might still run me out of business. He couldn't think how he'd be able to hold out if these cows got run off beyond recovery, and for sure, if there was shooting, which at this point seemed inevitable, the cows would scatter.

Well, by God, he told himself, he'd take out his share of these gunfighters. If he would up dead, or even just busted, at least he'd get a few of them first. Then he noticed the fat man in the lead of the gang across the way.

''Well, I'll be damned,'' he said.

''What?'' said Dusty.

''See that one in front?''

''The hefty one?''

''Yeah,'' said Starkey. ''That's Hiram Dancer. He's our sheriff. Slocum accused him of being on Berry's payroll. Looks like he's finally come out in the open.''

''That just means one thing to me,'' said Dusty.

''What's that?''

''He won't want to leave no witnesses alive to tell on him.''

''Well,'' Starkey said, ''someone's got to make the first move here. Should we do it or let them?''

''Let them,'' said Dusty. ''It's hard to ride and shoot straight at the same time.''

*   *   *

The sweat was running down Dancer's face by this time, and his shirt was soaked. His palms were so wet that he didn't know if he'd be able to hold on to his six-gun. But the standoff was getting to him. He was ready for something to happen, but he still hoped that Berry would come riding up at the last possible moment to relieve him of this unpleasant responsibility.

"Well, Sheriff?" the gunman next to him asked.

"What?" Dancer snapped back.

"We going to hit them or not?"

"You all move up in front of me," said Dancer.

The gunfighters moved ahead a little, and Dancer sat still, letting the line get in front of him. He might have a better chance of surviving the fight this way. Perhaps he could stay clear out of it. And since Berry had not showed, he wouldn't know about it anyhow. Dancer would give the orders, then hang back. If it started to look like things were going the wrong way, he could light out.

"Whenever you're ready," he said, "hit them, and hit them hard."

"All right, boys," said the gunman who had assumed the lead, "check your weapons."

Just then Dancer saw two riders coming hard from the direction of the Berry ranch. He couldn't recognize them yet, but he hoped that one of them might be Berry. Berry and Jo Jo, he thought.

"Hold it," he said. "Riders coming. Let's see who it is."

•   •   •

Slocum and Brandy had seen the two groups faced off at about the same time, and they both knew what was about to happen.

"Stay back," Slocum had said, and he had kicked his big 'Palouse into a run. Brandy spurred her mount on too and was doing her best to keep up.

"Like hell," she shouted. "I can stop them."

They rode hard, headed for the empty space between the two groups, hoping they could make it before someone fired a shot. Brandy waved and shouted.

Dancer at last recognized the two riders, and he did not know what to think. One was Slocum, but the other was Brandy Berry. What the hell, he wondered, was Brandy doing with Slocum?

"Hold on, boys," he said. "It's the boss's daughter."

On the other side, Starkey saw them coming.

"Dusty," he said, "it's Slocum. And Brandy's with him."

"Brandy?" said Dusty. "Who the hell is Brandy?"

"Ben Berry's daughter," Starkey said.

"Well, what the hell is she doing with Slocum?" Dusty asked.

"I'm damned if I know," said Starkey, shoving his hat back to scratch his head.

They didn't rein in their mounts until they were right between the two groups that were poised to start shooting at one another. Bringing their horses to a halt, they sat for a moment, breathing sighs of relief that no shot had yet been fired, and they looked from one group to the other.

"I see Dancer's over there with them," Slocum said.

"I'll take care of this," said Brandy, and she turned her horse and started walking it toward the gunfighters. Slocum held up a hand to tell Starkey and the others to stay back. Then he followed Brandy. They rode up to within a few feet of the gunfighters.

"It's all off, boys," she said.

"Where's your daddy?" demanded Dancer.

"He's dead, Sheriff," she said. "Killed by Jo Jo Darby. The ranch is mine now, so you boys are all on my payroll. I don't need gun hands, but if you want to go on working as cowhands, you can help Starkey and his crew drive that herd over to his place. If you don't want that kind of work, ride back to the ranch house and I'll pay you off. That's it."

The gunfighters looked at one another and shrugged. Finally one of them spoke up.

"I think I'll just ride on," he said. "I ain't no cowpuncher."

The others agreed with him.

"We'll wait for you back at the ranch, ma'am," the spokesman said, and they started riding. Dancer turned his horse to follow them.

"Hold it, Sheriff," said Slocum.

"What for?" said Dancer. "You heard Miss Berry. It's over."

"The war's over all right," said Slocum, pulling

out his big Colt, "but that ain't the same thing as a sheriff who's been on the payroll of a man who's been trying to run folks off their land. Toss that six-gun. I aim to put you in your own jail."

20

Seeing the gun hands ride away, Starkey rode across to where Slocum and Brandy remained with Dancer. Dusty and the cowboys slowly broke up their group and moved back to tend the herd. Starkey pulled up beside Brandy.

"What's going on?" he asked her.

"I told them that I'm the new boss, and I need only cowhands on the place," Brandy said. "I gave them the choice of collecting their wages and riding out or putting up their weapons to start herding cows. They went back to the ranch to wait for me to show up and pay them off."

"You mean it's over?" Starkey said. He had been all braced for a fight, and in a strange way, which he himself could not quite understand, he was disappointed.

"All over," said Brandy. "It's hard to believe, isn't it?"

"Yeah. It sure is." He looked at her, and her face was sad, but he knew that it was because of what had happened to her father.

"Well," she said, "I'd better get back to the ranch and pay those men off."

She turned her horse and started back toward the road. Slocum was keeping an eye on Dancer, but he also heard and saw what went on between Brandy and Starkey.

"Hey, boss," he said.

"What?" said Starkey.

"You care about that girl?"

"Well, hell," said Starkey. "Yeah. I care about her, I reckon."

"It seems to me this ain't no time to let her ride off alone."

"Well, what about Dancer there?" Starkey asked.

"I'll take him in," said Slocum.

"There's my cows."

"Panhandle can lead the boys to your place. They brought them this far without you. I reckon they can get them on home."

Starkey scratched his head and wrinkled his face. "I don't know," he said.

"Sam, you dumb bastard," said Slocum, "that girl just learned that her daddy was killed, and she didn't even have time to cry. The man who killed him kidnapped her and tried to rape her. I came along just in time to stop it.''

Starkey looked incredulous. His eyes opened wide and his mouth gaped.

''You mean,'' he stammered, ''just today? While ago? Who the hell was it?''

''It's what made me so late getting back here,'' said Slocum, ''and it was that damned Jo Jo. Who else?''

''Well, where is he? What happened?''

''I killed the son of a bitch and left him lying out there,'' said Slocum, ''and right now your girl is riding to meet up with a bunch of gunslingers. If she was my girl, I wouldn't want her to have to face them alone.''

''Yeah,'' said Starkey. ''You're right. You're right about that.''

He turned his horse and headed off at a gallop after Brandy. Slocum gave Dancer a hard look and gestured with the muzzle of his revolver toward the cowhands across the way.

''Ride over that way,'' he said. ''Go easy.''

Dancer nudged his horse and headed for where Dusty and the other cowhands waited, not knowing what had just happened over there on the other side. Slocum stopped Dancer within a few feet of the cowboys.

''Slocum,'' said Dusty, ''it's been a good while since I seen you, and right now you're a hell of a good sight.''

''Dusty Jones,'' said Slocum. ''It has been a while.''

''What's going on?'' Dusty asked.

"Well, sir," said Slocum, "the war's been called off. Berry's killed, and his daughter has fired the gun hands. The only thing left to deal with is this chicken-shit sheriff, and I'm hauling him into his own jail. I sent Starkey after the new owner of the Berry spread, 'cause she went alone to pay off the gunslingers. I reckon you boys can get the cows on over to Starkey's alone. Panhandle's been there. He knows the way."

"Hell," said Dusty, "I was planning to bed them down here for the night anyhow and drive them on in first thing in the morning. I'll be damned. So the war ain't going to happen?"

" 'Fraid not," said Slocum. "I hope you're not too disappointed."

"I reckon we'll manage," said Dusty.

"If you're sure you can handle them, then," Slocum said, "I'll ride on. I'll come back out in the morning and help you take them on home."

"We'll be looking for you," Dusty said.

Slocum looked at Dancer again.

"Head for town," he said.

Starkey caught up with Brandy before she had made it back to the ranch, and they rode along together the rest of the way. Mostly they were quiet. Starkey felt more than a bit awkward. What would he say to her? Her father had only just been murdered, but the old bastard had been trying to run Starkey off his own land. He didn't quite know how to deal with the situation.

He was glad the war was over, and he would be

able to live in peace and work his ranch. Did that mean he was glad that Berry was dead? That's exactly what had ended the war. The fact of Berry's death certainly didn't bother him any, or at least it wouldn't have, had it not been for Brandy. So he really didn't know what to say to her. He rode along beside her in silence.

When they reached the ranch house, they found the gun hands lounging around the porch. Brandy had a brief discussion with them so they all agreed on what they were owed. She went inside the house for a moment and returned with the money. When she had paid them off, they all rode away together.

"Well," said Starkey, "that was easy enough."

"I'm glad they're gone," said Brandy.

"Yeah."

"Sam," she said, "do you think we could locate all the folks that Daddy ran off? I mean, the former landowners in the valley."

"Well, I don't know," he said. "I know where some of them went. Chilly likely knows some more. I reckon we could. At least most of them. How come you want to find them?"

"I want to give them back their land," she said. "If they want it. If they want to come back. I want to make things right for what Daddy did to all those people. To you too."

"Aw, hell," he said. "He didn't do nothing to me. I still got my place. I'm all right."

"He sure gave you a lot of trouble," she said. "Caused some damage. I'll be glad to pay for it."

"You don't need to pay me for nothing, Brandy,"

he said. "What you're planning to do for the other folks—that's plenty enough. I sure do admire you for that. And I'll help any way I can. You call on me anytime. You hear?"

She shuffled her feet and turned so that she was directly facing Starkey. At first she looked at the ground. A moment later she looked up into his eyes.

"I don't know if I can handle this outfit by myself," she said. "I'm going to have to name someone foreman, I guess. I need to get a work crew to fix up the house. I don't know whether to pull cowboys off the range for that kind of work or not. I don't know—"

"I'll help you along," said Starkey.

"You've got your own ranch to take care of," she said, and she felt tears welling up in her eyes. What the hell did she have to say to him anyway?

"Aw, we can spare some time," he said. "Me and Slocum."

"Sammy," she said, and her voice was suddenly angry. "Sammy, do you love me or not? Do you want to marry me, or was I just a pleasant diversion to you?"

Starkey's face turned bright red. Brandy turned away from him. "I'm sorry," she said. "I shouldn't have said that. It's not a woman's place."

"Aw, Brandy," said Starkey, stepping up close behind her. "It ain't that. It's—I care a lot about you. I guess— Well, I do love you. I just didn't think that it'd look right, me with my little spread asking to marry you with your big one. It would look like I wanted your land."

"Your ranch and mine would fit together real well," Brandy said, "and besides, mine won't be nearly so big once I give all that land back to the rightful owners."

Starkey reached out and put his hands on her shoulders. He looked into her eyes. "Will you marry me?" he asked.

"Hell yes," Brandy said. "The sooner the better."

Slocum rode along slowly behind Dancer. The dirty lawman rode with his head hanging, his chin bouncing against his chest. They had passed the Berry ranch without a word having been exchanged between them. They were getting close to town. They were getting close to Dancer's jail.

"Slocum," Dancer said, "let me go. It's all over."

"I ain't letting you go," Slocum said.

"Well, I ain't letting you put me in jail."

"I don't see that there's a hell of a lot you can do about it," Slocum said.

The holster at Dancer's side was empty, but in an inside coat pocket he had an English Webley Bulldog pocket pistol. Slowly he eased his right hand underneath his coat. Slocum was riding behind him. He might get away with it. He did not intend to suffer the humiliation of being incarcerated in his own jail right there in Dead Dog for the citizens to come by and gape at. He did not want to stand trial and be sentenced.

He got his chubby hand on the Bulldog, and his palm was wet with sweat. He gripped the handle of the Webley, got his thumb on the hammer and his fat finger inside the trigger guard. He rode on for a bit in silence. Slocum didn't say anything. He must not suspect. Dancer knew that he would have to act quickly. His heart was pounding inside his chest.

He jerked the pistol out of his pocket, thumbing back the hammer at the same time, and he turned in the saddle, pointing the pistol back at Slocum. He snapped off a quick shot that whizzed close by Slocum's head. Slocum jerked out his Colt.

Dancer was thumbing back the hammer for a second shot when Slocum fired. The slug hit Dancer in the right armpit and came out on the left side of his chest. On its way through, it tore into his heart. He gasped out loud, dropped the pistol, and slumped. Then he slid slowly out of the saddle on the left side of his horse. His body landed in the road with a dull thud, and a small cloud of dust rose up around him.

Slocum rode into Dead Dog leading Dancer's horse with the fat sheriff's body slung across the saddle. He stopped in front of Alf Lomer's funeral parlor. When the gaunt undertaker stepped out onto the boardwalk and gave Slocum a questioning look, Slocum said, "It's Dancer. If there's anyone official left in town and they want some kind of an explanation, I'll be glad to give it to them. They can find me at the Dead Dog Saloon. At least for a little while."

He rode on down the street to the saloon, and he dismounted there and tied his stallion to the rail. Then he walked inside. There were a few customers in the place, but he didn't see Veronica. He moved on to the bar and leaned his elbows on it. Merle finished with another customer and walked over to Slocum.

"The usual?" Merle asked.

"Yeah," said Slocum, "and leave the bottle."

He dug some money out of his pocket, and when Merle put the bottle and glass in front of him, he shoved the money at Merle. Merle shoved it back.

"The boss says your money's no good in here, Mr. Slocum," he said.

"Where is the boss?" Slocum asked.

"She's upstairs in her room."

Slocum poured himself a drink and tossed it down. It had been a long, hard day, and he had killed two men. He poured a second drink and took a sip. Then he picked up the bottle in one hand and the glass in the other. He turned toward the stairs and looked up toward the landing. He took another sip of whiskey, then headed for the stairs.

He took them slowly, and at the top he walked down the hall to Veronica's door. Tucking the bottle under his arm, he tapped on the door with his knuckles. He heard Veronica's voice from inside the room.

"Who is it?"

He didn't answer. Instead, he tried the knob. It turned. He gave the door a shove and let it swing open, and he stood there in the doorway, leaning against the frame. Veronica was lying on the bed. She looked at him standing there, and she smiled, a soft, warm smile.

"Hello, lady," he said.

"Hello, big boy," she answered, "and I do mean big."

"Can I come in?"

"Who do you think I've been waiting for?"

He stepped inside the room, put his bottle and glass down on a table, shut and locked the door. He turned to face her again.

"How'd everything work out?" she asked.

He took off his hat and hung it on a peg in the wall.

"Satisfactory," he said.

"Does that mean you'll be moving on?" she asked.

"Oh," he said, "I think I'll hang around, at least for a few more days."

A special offer for people who enjoy reading the best 'Westerns published today.

WESTERNS!

NO OBLIGATION

Mail the coupon below

To start your subscription and receive 2 FREE WESTERNS, fill out the coupon below and mail it today. We'll send your first shipment which includes 2 FREE BOOKS as soon as we receive it.

Mail To: **True Value Home Subscription Services, Inc. P.O. Box 5235**
120 Brighton Road, Clifton, New Jersey 07015-5235

YES! I want to start reviewing the very best Westerns being published today. Send me my first shipment of 6 Westerns for me to preview FREE for 10 days. If I decide to keep them, I'll pay for just 4 of the books at the low subscriber price of $2.75 each; a total $11.00 (a $21.00 value). Then each month I'll receive the 6 newest and best Westerns to preview Free for 10 days. If I'm not satisfied I may return them within 10 days and owe nothing. Otherwise I'll be billed at the special low subscriber rate of $2.75 each, a total of $16.50 (at least a $21.00 value) and save $4.50 off the publishers price. There are never any shipping, handling or other hidden charges. I understand I am under no obligation to purchase any number of books and I can cancel my subscription at any time, no questions asked. In any case the 2 FREE books are mine to keep.

Name _____

Street Address _____ Apt. No. _____

City _____ State _____ Zip Code _____

Telephone _____

Signature _____
(if under 18 parent or guardian must sign)   12015-4

Terms and prices subject to change. Orders subject
to acceptance by True Value Home Subscription
Services, Inc.

JAKE LOGAN
TODAY'S HOTTEST ACTION WESTERN!

__SLOCUM AND THE LADY 'NINERS #194	0-425-14684-7/$3.99
__SLOCUM AND THE PIRATES #196	0-515-11633-5/$3.99
__SLOCUM #197: THE SILVER STALLION	0-515-11654-8/$3.99
__SLOCUM AND THE SPOTTED HORSE #198	0-515-11679-3/$3.99
__SLOCUM AT DOG LEG CREEK #199	0-515-11701-3/$3.99
__SLOCUM'S SILVER #200	0-515-11729-3/$3.99
__SLOCUM #201: THE RENEGADE TRAIL	0-515-11739-0/$4.50
__SLOCUM AND THE DIRTY GAME #202	0-515-11764-1/$4.50
__SLOCUM AND THE BEAR LAKE MONSTER #204	0-515-11806-0/$4.50
__SLOCUM AND THE APACHE RANSOM #209	0-515-11894-X/$4.99
__SLOCUM'S GRUBSTAKE (GIANT)	0-515-11955-5/$5.50
__SLOCUM AND THE FRISCO KILLERS #212	0-515-11967-9/$4.99
__SLOCUM AND THE GREAT SOUTHERN HUNT #213	0-515-11983-0/$4.99
__SLOCUM #214: THE ARIZONA STRIP WAR	0-515-11997-0/$4.99
__SLOCUM AT DEAD DOG #215	0-515-12015-4/$4.99
__SLOCUM AND THE TOWN BOSS #216 (3/97)	0-515-12030-8/$4.99